Mud Heaven

By

Margot Woods

This book is a work of non-fiction. Names of people and places have been changed to protect their privacy.

First published by AuthorHouse 05/18/04

ISBN: 1-4184-6360-4 (e-book)
ISBN: 1-4184-2690-3 (Paperback)
ISBN: 1-4184-2691-1 (Dust Jacket)

Library of Congress Control Number: 2004105023

Printed in the United States of America
Bloomington, IN

This book is printed on acid free paper.

"Come on in."

If I were a new dog owner bringing my dog to Margot Woods' Applewoods Dog Training, I might be surprised at a half acre of giant black walnut forest in the DC suburb of Laurel, Maryland, but probably I wouldn't notice. I'd be concentrating on dragging Spot through the sally port and praying Spotty didn't pick this occasion to humiliate me - again.

Up the ramp to the little green house in the forest. Spot has picked up my nervousness and is whining and pulling and objecting loudly and things are *not* going like I'd hoped. My knock inspires a zillion dogs inside, but they are promptly silenced and a handsome, dark-haired woman invites me into her tiny cluttered office which Spot could wreck in a heartbeat. There's a couch, her desk and chair and a metal folding chair for me. When I sit I grip Spot's collar in a grip of steel.

"Tell me about your dog," Margot asks, pleasantly. I don't figure she needs to know everything about Spot. "He's a fine dog and we love him to death," I say. "There's this teensy problem."

Spot growls. I really wish he wouldn't.

As the interview progresses I admit that yes UPS won't deliver to our house anymore and we can't invite friends over and it's a good thing Mother is forgiving and heals so quickly. I wish Margot wouldn't ask so many questions about me and my family. After all, Spot's the problem.

After half an hour or so, Spot's still growling, but I'm relaxed enough to notice the recent obedience ribbons on the walls. When I ask about them, Margot dismisses them with a smile.

Then, in a quiet conversational tone, she says, "Wrap. Come." And this sleek Doberman Pincher appears from somewhere in the back of the house, jumps the kiddy gate into the office and onto the couch. The Doberman looks at Spot in a manner I don't really care for and Spot doesn't either, but Spot stops growling. As Margot continues her questions I find it hard to minimize Spot's problems with that quiet, perfectly mannerly dog watching us.

Spot thumps his tail. If I had a tail I'd thump my tail too.

Some years ago, Margot Woods tried counting the dogs she's trained. At ten thousand she stopped counting. She's been training dogs for almost thirty years, she's usually overbooked and my fictional client will be lucky if Margot is willing to take Spot on. She's recognized as one of the top dog trainers in North America.

Margot trains dogs six am to six pm - except weekends when she has a couple night classes too. Her first dogs were Chows - who are notoriously difficult to train - and her Xany was a famous competitor in the AKC obedience ring. She switched to Dobermans because Chows are specialists. She needed five Chows to do what Wrap can do.

One of the things Wrap is doing, by the by, is evaluating Spot. By Wrap's reactions to Spot, Margot knows whether training him will be a piece of cake or a pain in the ass. Wrap is Margot's chief assistant, enforcer, training aide, service dog, demonstrator and is so brilliantly trained, Margot rarely offers a command. Wrap simply does what needs to be done.

Margot Woods likes jokes, good food, friends and generosity. She has no patience with nonsense - yours or mine.

She'll get Spot trained, and in the process she'll change your life. You'll learn to see dogs, you'll learn about yourself. You'll come to inhabit a denser, more interesting world.

And here you thought Margot Woods was *just* a dog trainer. Margot's a storyteller too. Enjoy.

Donald McCaig
Yucatec Farm

Donald McCaig is the author of *Nop's Trials* and *Eminent Dogs, Dangerous Men* among others. He and his wife Ann, run a sheep farm in the mountains of western Virginia.

Acknowledgements

This book started out with one story. The funny thing about the story is it almost didn't get in the book at all. Between the time I wrote that first story and the time I was to the point of writing the last story, things in my life had changed so much the first story no longer fit. I put it in anyway. It just didn't work. I took it out. It screamed in my head all day and all night until I gave in and put it back. It still didn't work, but rather than take it out all together, I re-wrote it.

Now instead of a story that really only told the beginning, the new story tells it all, from the beginning to the very end. With the new telling, the original title no longer worked, so that morphed into "The Grandest Butterfly of All". In a way, this book is as much a tribute to Delta as it is a tribute to all dogs. No, not true. This book is a tribute to him. Because of Delta, or the stories I wrote about him, I learned I could write; and even more, that other people liked to read what I wrote. Thank you, Delta Man.

While I am doing the thank you thing, I need to say thank you to all the people and dogs along the way that had faith in me, especially when I had lost all faith in myself.

Thanks goes to my first husband Steve. Without him I would never have made it this far. Rest in peace, Love, and continue to live in my heart. Thanks goes to my son Jesse, for putting up with a mother who can turn into a truly cranky old biddy at the drop of a hat or a muddy boot, as the case may be.

Thanks goes to Bill and Pat Schwartz for all their support and their help guiding me through the dark valley of correct spelling and punctuation while listening to me insist I couldn't write. Without their guidance I would never have made it past the first draft of the first group of stories. Thanks to their little Sheltie, Kensie for helping with "Behind Those Eyes". Thanks to Pam Loeb for finding her red pencil and managing to find mistakes I could have sworn weren't there the day before.

Thanks goes to Lauren Wilson, Delta Man, and Bitsy for agreeing to allow me to tell their story in more than one way.

Thanks goes to Carol Lea Benjamin for convincing me my stories really were worthy of publication and making me believe it.

Thanks goes to Barbara Nienaltowski, formerly of ABC Newsmagazine 20-20, for reading "The Little Dog That Could", the first Delta Man story and agreeing it was worth turning into a segment on 20-20.

Finally, in the list of individuals I need to thank I am saying a huge thank you to Amy Compton for her work editing all my scribbles, and to Donald McCaig for writing the introduction when all I asked him for was a few words for the back cover.

Thanks to all my students, both human and canine, for their belief in me even on my "poor woe is me" days. You guys are all great, and without you there would be no stories.

To Ming who taught me to walk and

To Lyric who helped me learn and

To Xaney who started me on the road I now walk

Table of Contents

"Every exit is an entry to somewhere."
Tom Stoppard

The Door to No Where

"Can you see it?" Watching her body language I shifted my weight ever so slightly and followed her intense gaze with my own eyes.

"Look carefully through the break in the trees."

Sure enough, just on the other side of the fence and a short distance back in the thick undergrowth there was a door. It was well hidden, and if not for the unwavering stare of my constant companion, I would have missed it altogether.

"Why the sudden interest?" I muttered. "It looks like it has been there for a very long time. Besides, it is just an old door, a door to nowhere." With a mood as dark and bleak as winter storm clouds, I turned back into the lane. We left the area, and I continued to trudge up the hill, following the lane toward the light of the house. All the while she just kept looking back over her shoulder and lagging behind. The last of the daylight faded just as we climbed the porch steps.

I knew it had to be morning because there was a hot breath in my face and I was being pushed off the bed. "Okay, okay, I'm getting up."

Reading my email and drinking a second cup of tea gave the day time to warm up. That and my companion's almost constant reminders about how a walk would do me good finally got me up, moving toward my boots and then the door. I was thinking how a nice <u>leisurely</u> stroll would be a pleasant way to start the day. But no, my partner had other plans.

"Hurry! Hurry up!" You gotta see this thing I found!" Back and forth she rushed, running up and taking my hand for a moment and then rushing off down the lane, only to turn around and run back again.

"Listen here," I was starting to get annoyed with her persistent badgering, "that door looks like it was just dumped and forgotten. I'm willing to bet it has been there for 50 years or more, and we have probably walked past it hundreds of times. So what's the big deal now? Besides, there's no way through the fence."

She glanced mournfully in my direction, shifted her weight from one side to the other and then turned back to the door. Her entire body appeared to be quivering with a need to get to that old door.

I gave in. I wasn't feeling as stiff as usual; the warmth of a day ablaze with fall color and warm sunlight helped me to agree with a plan to walk the fence line, our goal being to find a gate to the other side. After all, there had to be a gate somewhere in that long fence. Since the need for a gate had never come up before, we had never bothered to look for one. Today would be a good day to find it. I started walking down the lane with more purpose to my step than I had had in years. Yes, I thought I could see some wisdom in her desire.

Since I hadn't tried to walk this far for some time, I was forced to stop often to rest. She never would let me rest for as long as I really wanted, always insisting I get up and start moving again. Her persistent "move-along" nudges were a true show of good judgment, since I tend to stiffen up quickly. Twice I stumbled, and she was right there to steady me. Once when I dropped my cane I could have almost sworn she actually caught it before it hit the ground! Even with all her help and support, by noon I was sure I had reached a stage of total exhaustion. I was also beginning to think any hike of this length a very bad idea.

Shortly after noon, we reached a place where the lane ended abruptly. The way along the fence continued as a narrow path that was little more than an animal trail. Beside the trail the fence continued on through the woods as far as I could see through the thick vegetation.

I finally realized we were not going to find an opening any time soon. Spotting a small patch of sunlight with a comfortable looking log, I stopped to take stock of what we were doing. After a long rest in that warm spot, I managed to convince her we really needed to turn around and head back home.

Back at the house, I was too tired to do anything other than eat a few bites of supper, pull off my boots and fall across the bed. The last thing I remembered was the covers slowly being pulled up and a warm body stretching out next to mine. How in the world did she always know just where I needed warmth and where I needed pressure to help ease the pain? With that thought, darkness covered me like a furry blanket.

During the night Indian Summer left, chased away by the first of many winter storms. The next morning dawned cold and dank, a harbinger of the weather that continued to worsen into full winter. Cold, dark day followed pain-filled, cold, dark day. Most of the time I just stayed inside since it was so hard to move and I feared falling should I be foolish enough to venture outside. My steady, faithful partner would make quick excursions out to check on things each day. Then little by little I realized the days were getting longer again. There were days that didn't seem quite so cold; the ice and snow melted; early spring flowers were blooming in sheltered places.

One morning hot breath and steady nudging woke me to the fact that a truly nice day was about to start. Taking a couple of minutes to get my balance under control, I started for the bathroom and then the kitchen with the obligatory stop in the office to turn on the computer and check the mail. When I opened the door I realized it was going to be a wonderful warm, sunny day, and, yes a walk was definitely at the top of my list of things to do.

That morning walk became the first of what turned into a daily ritual. Every morning, rain or shine, we would walk at least as far as that place in the fence where we could look out and see the door. I became a student of that door. I took to studying it for hours on end. It was an old style door. The doorknob was low set, with chipped paint and a green tinge. The door itself had been painted at one time, but now weather and age made it impossible to tell what color it had been. Inset panels - set two long ones above two shorter ones - and the lack of any window made me think it had once been an inside door. Whatever sort it had been, it now rested out there in the woods and was beckoning me to come and investigate what lived on the other side. I said <u>lived</u> because I was coming to think of it as a door to somewhere.

My partner continued to insist we walk every day. Each day I tied a yellow ribbon to the fence to mark our progress.

"Hey, do you know what you are doing to me? I mean, do you realize you have managed to get me to walk further and further every day?"

"You know", I continued, "you are pretty slick with the way you get me to do stuff I think I don't want to do." She just glanced over at me, then picked up my cane and handed it to me.

We kept this schedule going all summer and into the fall. As the days started to get shorter and cooler again, I was faced with stiffening and pain. Having been without the worst of it for several months, the pain seemed just that much harsher when it returned. No longer could I walk all the way to the end of the line of yellow ribbons, and each day it was harder to get out of bed. Even with her help, her positive, upbeat attitude, just the very effort of getting out of bed left me shaking with pain and fatigue. For days at a time the struggle to do such a simple everyday task would take its toll and leave me weeping with frustration, certainly in no mood to venture out of the house. On days when I did manage go pull on my boots and go out, when we got to the place in the fence where we could both see the door, we stopped. It was so hard for me to even make it that far; going any farther was just out of the question. Yet the door continued to call.

That door - what was it about that door? In a certain light and when the angle was just right, I thought it looked as if it was opening just a little bit. In fact, I was sure it was opening. No longer just an old door, abandoned and forgotten.

The cold rains of fall came, and with the rain the stiffness and pain came crashing down on me. For days I was not able to walk to that spot, the place I had taken to thinking of as the door to <u>No Where</u>. As happens so late in the year, the weather changed again. For a few days it was cool, crisp and dry. It was much easier for me to get out of bed, and I was willing to go outside and even walk again. We headed straight for that spot just as soon as I was able to limber up enough to walk the distance.

Today was definitely different. Today my partner helped me sit on the log I had taken to using as my vantage point and instead of pacing up and down the fence line, she started to dig. All morning she dug, stopping to

4

take only a short break now and then. Into the afternoon she dug. By early evening when I insisted we had to head back for the house, she had managed to wear her nails down the quick. There was now a sizable hole under the fence. Tomorrow would be another day. Right now I needed rest, food, and a warm bed, and so did she.

Sure enough, the next morning I hurried as best I could to get through the slow morning rituals that my body demanded. Once I could move, albeit at a slow pace, we headed back to where the freshly dug hole huddled at the base of the fence.

Taking my seat on the log, I looked through the chain link. My eyes located the door, and I could have sworn there was a light streaming out around the edges. My partner started to dig almost at once. The dirt flew, and just a little before noon she broke through to the other side. At the same time she reached the other side I became aware of the air. It was getting colder and I could see storm clouds building up in the sky behind me.

"Great," I thought, "just great. Now she'll be able to go check out the door and I'm stuck here."

I was so wrong. A wave of guilt crashed over me for even daring to think she would ever consider leaving me behind. Instead, when she had wiggled to the other side of the fence, she turned around and started digging again. She was actually making the hole under the fence larger. The day stretched on, the air got colder and the wind began to pick up. With the sinking sun the area around us started to grow dark and snowflakes began to fall. It didn't much matter because I was no longer watching her dig, nor was I very much aware of the lack of light, the cold or the snow - because the door was definitely swinging open. I could see a warm and friendly light streaming out.

Satisfied with the size of the hole, my partner slid back under the fence and trotted over to me. She picked up my cane, handed it to me, and then turned sideways so I could grab her shoulders. The cane plus her pull managed to get me to my feet. It took no urging on her part to get me to limp to that hole under the fence. Using her as balance I slowly lowered myself to the now snow covered ground, and then, on my belly, followed her under the fence. Once on the other side she helped me to roll over and pull myself into a sitting position. Then clinging to her I managed to pull myself up. As soon as I was standing and stable she rushed back to the hole, zipped through to the other side and grabbed my cane. Poking and shoving and then coming back through and pulling, she managed to bring the cane to me. With it in my right hand and with her on my left, we made our way to that door and its light and warmth.

I looked down at her and she, looking up at me, seemed to grin and her stump of a tail was just a blur as it wagged with pleasure. With my hand lightly touching her neck the two of us stepped through that door, going from No Where to Some Where.

"People only see what they are prepared to see."
Ralph Waldo Emerson

The Observers

If you have ever trained a dog in a public park, it's likely you have met at least one of the observers. When I first started training dogs we used to call them "the wincers", and while their name has changed, they haven't. They still tend to lurk around just looking for someone with a dog that is well behaved. Then they zero in to badger and bully. So just who and what are they? This is a story about a single Saturday in late spring and one such observer.

I had four dogs in need of training, and they really needed to be trained in a more public setting than the two small parks I tended to favor. So when I got up in the morning and realized what a gorgeous day it was going to be, I couldn't think of a better plan than to load all the dogs in the back of my van and head for the park with the lake. Not merely a lake mind you, but one with ducks, geese, children and lots of foot traffic - made to order as a great training spot and one that was sure to present the dogs with lots of opportunities to say "no" to distractions.

I tend to stay away from such places until the dogs I am training are almost finished with the beginning phases of their training. Sad to have to do that, because the dogs would benefit so much from being able to train around that lake right from the very beginning. But I wander in my story in the same way I ended up wandering for a large part of the training time that sunny Saturday.

Pulling into the parking lot, I found a shady spot to park the van and unloaded my first dog. Because he was the youngest of the four, had the least amount of training and the shortest attention span, I figured to work him first. This early in the morning the park wasn't crowded with a lot of people. This made the job of staying on top of his response to distractions much easier. Opening his crate door I called him out. After he sat, I checked to make sure his ecollar was turned on. Then, snapping a fifteen-foot longe line on his plain buckle collar, I gave him a heel command and started down the path to the lake. Rally was a young Doberman with so much energy it sort of leaked out of him and caused him to look like a drop of cold water in hot fat. No way was he physically or mentally able to walk in a calm and controlled fashion when he first started out in the morning. The ride in the back of the van plus the additional heady smells wafting up from the lake had managed to crank him up to just below explosion point.

Our progress down the path must have been ridiculous looking.

Me: (tap on the remote) Rally, heel.

Rally: lunge forward about ten steps.

Me, coming to a standstill: (tap on the remote) Rally, come.

Rally: leaping in the air to execute a tight turn and then charging me.

Me: (tap on the remote) Rally, sit.

Rally: leaping in the air to lick my nose and then slamming into a sit position.

Me: stepping forward again with a (tap on the remote) Rally, heel.

In this fashion it took us the better part of thirty minutes to cover a distance that would normally only take about five minutes to walk at a rather slow pace. Rally was going to make this a patience-trying session. It was one of those times when I found myself repeating over and over again, "Only a fool gets mad about winning, and I am going to win. I am not a fool, so I will not get mad."

I have to practice what I preach to my students, after all! I am always reminding someone that they are smarter than their dog. Being human they are smarter, this means they are going to be able to figure out a way to let the dog know what is required. Since once the dog understands what is required the job will get done, the student will be winning and so will the dog. Only stupid people get mad at the thought of winning. I don't have any stupid students. They chose me as their instructor, didn't they? So of course it just naturally follows that no student of mine will get mad at their dog. Or so I tell them. Taking thirty minutes to cover a distance that should only take five minutes is one of those times when it would be really easy to get mad.

Once we made it to the lakeside, I could see far enough of a distance in both directions to give Rally an "okay" and release him to run, knowing that a good run would make it much easier for him to concentrate on the commands I planned to work on later in the day. Yes, I am very much aware of the leash laws. And, yes, I am very much aware that by turning Rally loose the way I did, I was breaking those leash laws. But darn it, my taxes help pay for the upkeep and maintenance of that lake and park. There were no other people out and about, and I was working a dog that was under my control. Besides, I was also working with the political powers that be on making changes in those laws. That's not an excuse mind you, but it is an explanation for why I would continue to work dogs off leash when they are ready for that responsibility.

Hearing the okay, Rally literally launched himself a good eight feet through the air and hit the ground going full speed. I let him run about a hundred feet before tapping on the remote button and giving a rather loud, "Rally, Come." I had to tap and call a total of three times before my voice was able to override the joy of hurling through the air at top speed. Rally gave a yip of frustration, whirled around in mid-air and headed back at me at the same speed he had been traveling away from me. Notice how I said he headed back at me rather than saying he headed back to me.

There is a big difference between the actions involved in the "to" and the "at". I very much wanted a "to" and I most certainly didn't want an "at". That being the case, I started tap, tap, tapping on the button on the remote for his ecollar.

Tap, tap, tap, as I gave a sit command. Tap, tap, tap, as I repeated the same sit command. Nothing. Nada. He didn't even slow down a little bit. I repeated the tap and command sequence again, only this time I used the button for a medium level tingle on the ecollar. Nothing. The fourth time I used the high level as I ran though the same sequence. Four times I had to do that while increasing the stimulation level before it dawned on him that he really needed to slow down a bit and think about what he was going to do next.

Happily for the both of us, my timing was great and I got him to slow down, focus on me and actually slide into a sit before he crashed headlong into me. I just grinned at him, slid my hand down the side of his neck in a gentle stroke and released him to run again. Over and over again we practiced that release, run, call, return and sit until he no longer had a bad case of the twitches. Now I could put him back in the crate in the van for a rest and start working with the next dog.

The morning wore on and the number of people around the lake continued to climb. Each dog that I took out to work had a higher level of training and was comfortable with the level of distractions the people, the ducks and the geese could throw at them. By the time I was working the fourth dog, the crowd around the lake was beginning to approach Friday evening rush hour traffic on the beltway. Sure was a good thing I had worked Rally early. There was no way it would have been acceptable to allow him a good run, even if off leash running had been allowed.

A funny thing about working a trained dog off leash in public. People see what they want to see or what they expect to see and not necessarily what is. Since I was working on a close, tight heel position with all three of the other dogs, I guess it must have looked okay. I always carry a leash in my hand - you never know when it might be needed. Two of the dogs had progressed in their training to the point where they were no longer wearing an ecollar for training. In fact, they weren't wearing an ecollar at all, and the last dog I worked wasn't wearing any sort of collar. She was, as we like to say, working naked. A state that I very much doubt anyone other than the two of us was aware of, since Border Collies do have enough coat to hide a number of collars.

When I finished working with May, the Border Collie I took a break, checked the water levels in all the crate water buckets then dug into the cooler for some lunch and a cold Coke. While I was eating lunch a pack of young boys stopped by and started asking questions about the dogs.

"What's that little black dog?" The kid looked to be about twelve and sort of hung over the handlebars of his bike. "It sure is funny looking. What happened to its tail?"

He was talking about the Schipperke sitting in the small crate that could be seen through the open side doors. Ber had come to me originally as a totally out of control young dog with a bite history. Now, a year and much hard work later, he was happy, bouncy, obedient, and fun to work. His owners had both worked hard and with the help of an ecollar and my guidance had really turned him around. Owners on vacation, Ber was getting some additional training while staying with me.

"Oh, that little guy is called a Schipperke. He is supposed to look like that. In the land were the Schipperke originated, they worked and still work on the barges as a ratter and alarm dog. Would you like to meet him?" One of my mottos is never, not ever should you pass up a good training opportunity.

With that, two of the boys plus the speaker put their bikes down and moved up to the van. The fourth boy stayed on the path and made no attempt to come closer. From his behavior I figured he was probably afraid of dogs. While looking at him, I happened to notice a woman standing just a short way down the path and watching us. I had noticed her quite a few times during the morning and was starting to wonder about her. The sour expression on her face was enough to tell me she didn't like what she was seeing. Since she was keeping her distance and hadn't spoken, I chose to ignore her.

Turning my attention back to the three boys, I said, "Before I get Ber out for you to see I need to explain the rules. I would be so happy to have you help a little bit with his training. Think you'd like that?"

The boldest of the trio moved up closer. "Yeah, what do you want us to do? You attack training that big one? Will we get to see him bite somethin'?"

Now this is one of the parts of my job I have a love/hate feeling about. Kids don't have any idea how to approach or behave around a dog these days, (of course some of them are at a total loss as to how to behave around other humans, so I guess I really shouldn't feel like I am being singled out!)

"No, I am not going to have any of the dogs bite anything other than their food at dinner tonight. That isn't what owning or training a dog is all about. What is going to happen is that when I get Ber out of his travel crate, I am going to tell him to sit right here beside me. Then you can see him a little better, and he can see you. What happens after that will be pretty much up to you."

The smallest of the three, a little blond-haired fellow who looked to also be the youngest of the group spoke up, "Wha'd ya mean, up to us?"

11

"Well, if you are quiet and calm in the way you move, I will go ahead and let him out of the van. Then I will start by having him sit so you can take turns petting him. If that goes well, I will then show you how to do the exam part of what we call a "stand for exam". After that, well, we will just have to see. Interested?"

I got three eager yes responses. I turned to look at the fourth boy just in time to see him back as far off the path as the lake would allow. He then placed his bike between himself and the rest of us. So I was right, he was afraid of dogs. Being this close to some trained dogs just might help to change his mind. I chose to pretend I hadn't noticed his movement. I also noticed that the woman I continued to see had now been joined by what appeared to be a crony. Neither of them looked very friendly, and they were whispering to each other as they watched what I was doing. I just figured I would continue to mind my own business and trust that they would mind theirs.

Making sure Ber's ecollar was turned on I started to jump him out of the van only to stop because all three boys demanded to know just what the funny collar was and why there was a flashing red light. Now I was starting to move into an area where I really feel at home, teaching. "That is an ecollar he is wearing. It is also called an electronic training collar. Would you like to try it?"

They all giggled and then the first boy stepped up with his chest stuck out and said, "Sure, why not? What's it do?"

I got another ecollar out of my equipment bag and turned it on. I let them watch me as I held the contact points in my hand and started tapping the buttons on the remote. "This remote works a little bit like a TV remote. It sends a signal to the collar, and then the collar sends a signal the dog. Who wants to feel the signal?"

Much to my surprise the first boy stepped back and said, "Not me, you ain't gonna shock me with that thing."

At that the little blond stepped up and stuck out his hand, "Not scared, I wanna try."

So I handed over the collar and showed him how to let it rest on the palm of his hand. With the remote set on the lowest setting I tapped the button. He didn't even blink. "Did you feel anything?"

"Feel anything? You didn't do anything, did you?"

"Yes I sent you a signal on the lowest setting." And with that, I turned the remote up one level and hit the button again. The kid blinked.

"Did you feel that?"

"I'm not sure. Do it again."

So I did. Again he blinked but didn't do anything else. I hit the button again and this time he said, "Nah, I don't feel anything. Does it even work?"

I moved up the dial one more notch and hit the button. This time he jumped and then started laughing. "Do it again. Do it again! It feels real funny!"

So I hit the button a couple more times, and the entire time he just kept on laughing. The second boy, who up to this point had not said a word, simply held out his hand. So I reclaimed the collar and put it on his hand.

I turned the intensity dial back to zero and started tapping the button. I went up a notch, then another notch and then another notch. The hand twitched but other than that there was nothing. All the boys were now real quiet. "Well, what do you want to do?" I asked him.

"Go up one more," he said in a quiet voice.

I did and his entire arm jumped. With that he just grinned and handed back the collar. "Pretty neat", was all he had to say.

At this point the first boy all but grabbed the collar from me. "Hey, take it easy! You'll get your chance."

With the collar resting on his palm I started the entire process all over again. Zero, one, two then three. I knew from the way his eyes twitched that he had felt something on two, but he neither moved nor spoke. On three his hand twitched, and I stopped.

"Is that as high as Joey went?"

"Yes."

"Keep going."

"Are you sure?"

"Ya."

"Okay." And I turned the dial up to four. Hit the button and watched him grit his teeth, grin and announce it was nothing.

Locking eyes with me, he grinned and said, "Go higher."

I just shook my head and grinned back as I moved the dial up to 5 and hit the button. His whole arm jumped wildly, and the ecollar flew off. All the boys started laughing, shouting and jumping around and throwing punches at each other. The feeling I got from them was that the leader of the little pack had just maintained his status and maybe even moved up a couple more notches. Boys - what can I say?

The entire time all this foolishness had been going on, Ber had been sitting quietly by my side and watching them with much interest. This didn't surprise me at all since I have always been convinced that all Schipperkes were just young boys that somehow got stuck in the body of a small, black whirlwind of a dog.

I looked up just before I jumped Ber out of the van and don't you know, the two women had moved much closer and were now positively glaring at me from behind a car that was parked just two cars away from me. Then it hit me. They were observers of the worst sort, and I was going to be really lucky if I managed to get out of there without having to listen to a barrage of unpleasant words. Didn't matter, because at this point I was fully committed to this small pack of boys and their education. Over the next fifteen minutes or so the boys learned how to approach a dog, how to pet one, how to not pet one, and when to leave a dog alone. Not only did they try out their newly learned skills with Ber, but I had them do the same thing with May, then with Troll, a mixed breed of unknown ancestry. Finally I figured they were good enough at what they were doing for me to get Rally out.

I was working things pretty much based on the size of the dog. Having started with the smallest I had with me I had slowly worked my way up to the largest. Rally, sleek, black and tan, ninety plus pounds and twenty-nine inches at the shoulder was by far the largest of the dogs and pretty impressive looking. He was also young and had the least amount of training. This was going to be a really good test for all concerned.

Before I jumped Rally out of the van, I checked his ecollar to make sure it was working and then attached a longe line to his flat buckle collar. The boys were watching what I was doing with much interest and had all moved a little closer together.

When I jumped him out of the van, the boys got really quiet. I will say one thing for them, they all held their ground and didn't jump around, yell or do any of the things I call acting stupid. Good. That meant I had done my job of teaching. Out of the corner of my eye, I noted the fearful boy. He had at some point managed to gather up the other bikes and stack them in front of himself, but he had stayed; and considering his overall behavior, I took that to be a good sign. Seeing him caused me to remember the observers.

Looking around I didn't spot them at first and then realized that they were now standing only a short distance away. They had also stopped hiding behind a car. I continued to ignore them.

Once Rally was out of the van, I gave a tap on the button and a sit command. Rally sat and the leader of what I was now thinking of as my little pack wanted to know what number he was on. Glancing at the dial I said, "Three."

"That's all? He's big and he is only on a three. I took a five." Chest puffed up and the strutting started.

"Ah, but you weren't trying to learn anything, and that makes a big difference. It doesn't have a thing at all to do with how much you can "take", and it has every thing to do with how it can help you focus on a task."

"Huh, well, he should be meaner than that. My Dad says dovermens are mean. He sure doesn't look mean to me."

"He isn't. Besides which, what good would he be if he was mean? You wouldn't be able to pet him. I wouldn't be able to work him. He would have to stay at home, locked up behind a high fence all the time. There wouldn't be any point in even having him, now would there?"

If nothing else that sure shut the kid up for the time being. And while things were quiet, I took the time to heel Rally out onto the path and tell him to stand. Again, the boys were interested in how and what I was doing with the ecollar.

"Well, I tapped the button as I said heel and I remembered to step off on my left foot to help Rally learn when to move with me. Then I stopped on my right foot as I tapped the button and told him to stand. Now I am going to tap the button and tell him to stay. And you are going to come up and do with him just like you did with the other dogs. Think you can do that?"

Sure enough, all three of them were able to do a complete exam, head, shoulders, and back, just the way they had done with the smaller dogs. I then thanked them and pointed out that I needed to get back to training. After assuring them they were free to stay and watch as long as they wanted and explaining that once I started working I wouldn't be able to answer any more questions until I was finished, I heeled Rally back to the van so I could exchange the longe line for a shorter, and very lightweight piece of cord. Next I put the longe line back in my equipment bag, pulled out a pack of cards, and began to shuffle them.

This caused the boys to start laughing and of course they wanted to know if I was going to teach the doverman to play cards. I just smiled. Much as I wanted to at least teach them how to say Doberman, I figured I had done enough for the day, and it was time to move on.

My lesson plan for the day with Rally called for me to spend the next half hour working on the moving stand, moving sit, and moving down, and to tie them together with the heel command. In order to insure some sort of randomness to the work pattern, I would use the pack of cards. All the red cards would call for a sit. All the black cards would call for a down. All the face cards would call for a stand. Then I would either return to him or call him to heel depending on my mood at the moment. I got busy working, and soon my world pretty much narrowed down to the dog, the distractions and the job. Tap, heel. Tap, stand and continue moving. Stop, pull out another card. Return to him and again, tap heel. Slowly we worked our way through that entire pack. There had been very few mistakes, and I was feeling really good about the entire day's work. Time to call it quits, load up and head for home.

Heeling Rally back to the van, I moved passed the car parked three down from us. Almost out of nowhere popped the observer from earlier in the day. "I'm a dog trainer, and that is the dumbest dog I have ever seen." With that she turned and walked away. Guess I should be thankful she didn't say anything earlier in the day. You know what? I am still trying to figure out what on earth she was talking about.

"It is not because things are difficult that we do not dare, it is because we do not dare that they are difficult."
Seneca

Sara's Fault

It really was all Sara's fault but it is wrong to say it quite that way. I mean, fault implies something wrong. There was nothing wrong with what Sara did, in fact she pretty much did everything right; and <u>that</u> is why I keep insisting it was her fault I took a deep breath and stepped into a new phase of my life.

The ringing of the phone caused me to stop in my tracks and head for the office.

"All Good Dogs. May I help you?"

"I can't believe we listened to you,' the voice on the other end was all but screaming.

"Huh?" I know, that's not one of my brightest or most clever responses, but what can I say? I mean, how should you respond to a statement like that? And to top it off I didn't even recognize the voice.

"I spent years saving up for that table and now it is ruined and it is all your fault and I hate that dog and I am never going to speak to my husband again and you should have to pay for the table top and I think I am going to make my husband get rid of the dog and why would you tell him to do something like that?"

Wow, I didn't realize that one person could get that many words out without ever stopping to take a breath. The trouble was, I still didn't have a clue as to who this was, nor did I have a clue as to what on earth she was talking about.

Sticking my neck out, in my most pleasant voice, I asked for her name and please would she mind starting from the very beginning.

"Start from the beginning?" she shouted, "I did start from the beginning. He jumped his dog up on my coffee table and now the top is in ruins. And HE said you told him to do that."

"Please, first tell me your name, and then tell me your dog's name." I figured at least that would give me some place to start.

"Oh, I'm sorry, it's just that I am so upset about my table I can't believe he would do something so stupid; I can't believe you would tell him to do something so… so… so…,"

"Slow down, you still haven't told me who you are."

"This is Mardi Dupont and it's my husband's dog."

"Okay, Mardi, what is your husband's dog's name?"

"Ice Breaker, and we call him Ice." Finally, I was getting somewhere with this conversation. In fact, I was now thinking I might even be able to be a participant.

"Ice is a nice dog, and last time I saw both your husband and the dog they were working just great. How about you tell me all about the table?"

I had earned my living training dogs and teaching dog training for many years and then took a break. Actually, I thought of it as going into semi-retirement. I still trained my own dogs and accepted a few clients now and again. Then my circumstances changed, and I found myself in the position of having to go back to full time training and teaching. Now back to the full time stuff, I was once again struggling with the questions of how do you teach someone to train their dog and at the same time not become a marriage counselor, home improvement specialist and child-rearing guru all rolled into one?

This time the problem was one of marriage counselor and home improvement specialist. Darn it, all I really wanted to do was train dogs.

18

"My table, my beautiful table!" Mardi raged on. "We've been married for almost 4 years and that table is our very first nice piece of furniture. I saved and saved for it, and he went and jumped Ice up on the top and now it has deep scratches in it."

"So what was Marc trying to get Ice to do? Did you ask him? Wait a minute here, did this happen last night during the football game?"

"Yes it did", she said slowly, "the commercials came on and he started telling Ice to 'place,' and then Ice started running around the room in circles and finally jumped up on the coffee table."

The muddy waters were starting to clear just a little bit. "Mardi, was Ice being a pest?"

"Well, yes, he has gone from running away, trying to pick fights and never wanting to be near us, to always being underfoot and in the way. All Marc was trying to do was to get Ice to go to his bed. Instead, the stupid dog ruined my table."

Slowly, ever so slowly, I managed to pull her side of the story out of her. Marc had been sitting in front of the TV happily watching the game, and Ice was just being a big, friendly pest. Bored with the lack of activity, Ice decided to start some of his own. He brought Marc toy after toy with no success. Then he started nudging Marc. Finally when halftime started, Marc got up and found the remote that activated Ice's electronic training collar, and the games began.

The next afternoon, the shrill peal of the phone jerked me out of a doze. "All Good Dogs, may I help you?"

"Yeah, help me and Ice get out of trouble." Poor Marc, both he and Ice were still getting the cold shoulder from Mardi.

"So tell me what happened? How on earth did you ever manage to end up with Ice on top of the table?"

"Well, I was watching the game, and Ice was really being a pain. He kept getting in the way of the TV. I told him to down, but he wasn't really listening. I finally remembered you said if I didn't have the remote in my hand, and I wasn't pushing the button, it wouldn't work. I did the dumbest thing, I pointed the TV remote at him, and told him to sit. He actually sat!"

Laughing, I pointed out it was pretty obvious that some training was taking place, I just wasn't sure what kind or who was being trained. "Go on, what happened next?"

"Well, when halftime started, I figured I really should go get the collar remote to practice that 'place' command you have been after us to work on."

"And?"

"And I got the remote, but I didn't bother to get a leash, and it never occurred to me that I needed to look around at all the stuff in the room."

"Meaning?"

"Well, the dog bed I am using for his place was at the end of the sofa, on the other side of the coffee table. I tried to explain to Mardi that all that happened was that Ice exercised his options and tried out using the coffee table for his place instead of the bed. After all he doesn't even like hard surfaces so why would he want to jump on the table instead of going to the bed? I almost think he did it on purpose, just to make trouble."

"Ice wasn't trying to get you in trouble with Mardi, but you are right about one thing, he was most definitely trying out all his options. Now do you understand why you need to have a leash on him and really take a good look at the surrounding environment <u>before</u> you start to work on this command? Remember, you are still in the teaching phase of Ice's training."

"Yeah, and I suppose you are going to tell me I should have turned off the TV and really worked Ice. That's what Mardi said."

"Surprise! I think you should leave the TV on and learn to concentrate on your dog when there is a need, no matter what the distraction happens to be. When you are requiring Ice to give you his full concentration you have an obligation to return the courtesy. And Marc, call the company you bought the table from, and get someone to come in and refinish the top. Then order a heavy piece of glass cut and beveled to fit it. Trust me, it is easier on the nerves in the long run. Oh, and tell Mardi that all Ice is really doing is teaching the two of you how to become good parents one day." We said good-bye; I hung up the phone and then headed off to deal with my next client.

Lucy with her Standard Poodle, Comfort, was my next client. (Or should I say student, since Lucy was in the process of training a second dog with me.) Then again, maybe I really should say friend since our relationship had blossomed into a friendship between herself and her husband, and myself and my husband. (But that is another story for another time.)

"You're moving too fast for her. Let's take a step back and work the command just a little closer to the platform for right now. Give Comfort more guidance until she understands what you want."

Lucy walked Comfort around for a few minutes and then approached the platform sitting in the middle of the training floor.

A small, 18" x 24" x 2" high wooden platform was what I routinely used to introduce a dog to the concept of "place". Place is the command used to send the dog away from the handler. With each dog we start out teaching a come or recall command and then after a week of practice we add a sit command. Come brings the dog to us and sit stops the dog in motion. The third week we teach a place command so the dog can be sent away from us to a new location.

It is much easier for a dog to learn to execute this command when the location they are being sent to is different from the surrounding area. In this case, by using an elevated, wooden platform the dog is able to gather information through the pads of his feet as well as with his eyes, nose and the guidance given via ecollar, regular collar and a leash. It normally only takes a relatively few number of repetitions before the dog starts to show understanding of the command by moving ahead of the owner and getting on the platform without help.

"Comfort, place" and with that Lucy pushed the button on the remote and simultaneously helped Comfort step on the low platform. By the third repetition, Comfort was relaxed about moving towards the platform. By the fifth repetition, she was starting to move toward the platform on her own when she heard the command, "Place".

"Lucy, you've done five repetitions approaching from that direction, now you need to change the direction of your approach and do five more repetitions. Remember to have Comfort remain on the platform for different lengths of time. Don't be in too much of a hurry to let her leave."

Lucy was just completing the last of what was a total of 20 repetitions when my phone started to ring. "Okay, take a break while I answer the phone," and I headed for the office.

"All Good Dogs, may I help you?"

"My dog just bit my husband and the vet said I should call you."

Hearing that statement on the other end of the phone line I knew I was back, to both training and teaching others how to train dogs. Just that now days, I was finding the work less physical and a whole lot more mental. You know, I still say it was Sara's fault. I had been so sure I couldn't train anymore after a serious knee injury, then I saw Sara. Watching her work made me realize that her training was more a mental thing than a physical one, and I knew I could handle that part. So here I am trying to be a dog trainer when sometimes I think people really only want a family counselor or a home improvement specialist or both.

And about Sara, in case you're wondering. Sara was a young, small, leggy Labrador. A shiny black bullet of a dog with a tail that never stopped its furious wagging and a tongue that constantly lolled out in a big grin. She took the commands being shot at her in machine gun fashion and never missed a beat. See, she really was perfect in the execution of her job the day I first saw her, and that is why I continue to maintain it really was all her fault that I not only went back to being a full time dog trainer but a dog trainer whose first choice in training equipment was an electronic training collar.

Sara had been totally trained with an electronic collar and she was something to behold. Sometimes called a remote training collar and most often these days just referred to as an ecollar. It is a training aid that has totally changed the way dogs and people can communicate. The good quality ecollars have a smooth stimulating feel that is very much the same as the feel of one of those muscle-stimulating units a chiropractor uses on your back to help your muscles relax.

In fact, the time I hurt my back and had to see a chiropractor, as soon as I realized just where he was putting the touch pads on my back, I actually used one of my ecollars on the same spot when I was having a problem and needed some relief from the pain. So you see, an ecollar is just a tool, and how you use it makes all the difference in the world.

After watching Sara work, seeing how her trainer handled the ecollar, I realized there was no need for me to worry about the fact that I could no longer do the running, jumping, twisting, sudden turning and, fast stopping I had previously engaged in while training a dog. Mind you, I still miss being able to do all those things and at the same time I sure am glad there is now another way. Besides which, it really is not only less strenuous but gentler for both dog and human. Sara's fault? Yes, yes indeed.

Life may not be the party we hoped for, but while we're here we should dance.
Unknown

Squirrels

Different people view squirrels in different ways. If you are not a homeowner you may see a squirrel as a cute, maybe funny and some times entertaining slice of nature. If you are a homeowner responsible for the care and upkeep of a home you may have had to deal with the problems and the damage a squirrel can do to a home in one short season. Paying the cost of repairs to your home means you aren't likely to find them at all amusing. Of course, there is a third category, a category not used very often these days. You might view them as food and clothing.

I happen to fall into the second category, because over the years I have had to deal with some pretty extensive, expensive damage done by marauding armies of squirrels. Call them squirrels if you must. I see them as tree rats, rats with furry tails, thieves who come into my yard and steal the nuts from my walnut trees. Mind you, I wouldn't mind if they came, ate some nuts and left. But no, they come as an army; they only eat half the nut and then throw the remainder at the dogs. If that wasn't bad enough they break into the attic of my house and chew on all sorts of things they have no business chewing on. Things like the insulation, the wiring, the very house itself. Left to their own devices I suspect the fur tailed tree rats would eat a portion of the house and then burn the remainder down around my ears.

When I first moved into this place I had two dogs that realized the dangers inherent in allowing squirrels free reign. Working as a team they did a wonderful job of keeping things under control for me. Their teamwork was marvelous to behold. One would dance and spin, running from tree to tree while doing this wondrous dance. The other would wait patiently until it happened.

"What happened?" you ask.

"The fool tree rat would get dizzy and fall out of the tree." I answer.

"Then what?" you ask.

"Why the obvious of course. The two dogs would at once pounce and in less time than it takes to blink there would be one less of those critters around to chew the insulation from the wires in the attic. Good riddance," said I.

Then came the day when the older partner left for the Rainbow Bridge. This meant the job was going to somehow have to be done by one dog. At first things went well. Somehow she managed to dance, spin, twirl, leap and still catch the squirrels that fell from the trees.

However over time a serious problem developed. Now mind you, it didn't happen over night. No, not at all that fast, in fact it took a couple of years before things really began to fall into place.

Nature calls for the hunter to be very patient, to not become discouraged by lack of success over long periods of time. The hunted, managing to avoid capture, becomes bolder and bolder. In this case, since one dog really couldn't do both the enticing and the catching a change was bound to happen. Alone and without the aid of a hunting partner, she was at the mercy of those furry tailed tree rats.

The squirrels quickly learned to sit up in the trees, chattering and screaming vile comments at the dog. Meanwhile the dog, lacking any sort of meaningful backup, learned to enjoy the dance. After all, it wasn't as if the squirrels were needed for food and since the dance was sufficient to keep them in the trees and keeping them in the trees made it very difficult for them to get to the house, the job was getting done. It just wasn't getting done with the same efficiency as in earlier days.

The dog sang. The dog danced. She twirled. She leapt and spun under the trees. She was a constant blur of motion spinning and dashing from tree to tree. This was something to be done for hours each and every day. Everyone was reasonably content with the status quo. Until the day IT happened. Who knows why IT happened. For those watching it was pretty obvious that the dog was doing the squirrel dance with unusual vigor. The twirls and spins were faster than usual. The leaps were definitely higher and the dog almost seemed to hang suspended in mid-air for a few seconds at the top of each leap. The squirrel remained unseen and unheard.

The dog ran from tree to tree, higher and higher she leapt and she had even added a new move. She was somehow twirling in mid-air. Quite something to watch and it caused me to comment, "You know, I don't think it is about squirrels anymore. I think it's all about the dance."

"No way," was the response from others watching. "She really does want to catch a squirrel."

At that very moment, down from the heights of the tree fell a something. From where we were standing it looked sort of like a child's hat. This object hit the dog square on the head just as she reached the top of one of her leaps. The dog yelled with annoyance. She landed, the thing fell off of her head and she continued to finish the twirl that always followed the leap.

Meanwhile, the thing lay on the ground, flat and unmoving. The dog took another leap and started the spin that went with the leap. The thing on the ground became a lump that grew a head. Then it turned into a squirrel. It stood up and shook itself. The dog landed and started the spins that always followed the two-leap sequence. The squirrel stared at the dog for a split second. It then turned, scampered around the tree to the far side where it proceeded to run right back up the trunk.

And the dog, what about the dog? In mid spin, something clicked in her brain. She stopped, froze and then bolted to the far side of the tree. Too late, very much too late, as the squirrel was already out of reach. Standing with paws stretched up as high as possible on the trunk, the dog watched the squirrel run higher and higher only stopping when a solid branch was reached. She heaved a loud sigh, put her front feet back on the ground, stood there for a moment and then…

And then the dance went on.

See I told you it was about the dance and not about the squirrels. Besides which, someone once told me squirrel pie really wasn't very tasty.

It was many and many a year ago
In a kingdom by the sea
That a maiden there lived, whom you may know
By the name of Annabelle Lee
And this maiden she lived with no other thought
Than to love and be loved by me.
Annabelle Lee
Edgar Allan Poe

Annabelle Lee

This Annabelle Lee was no maiden nor did she live in a kingdom by the sea. There was even a goodly amount of doubt as to just how much she loved anyone or anything other than herself.

There was water, just not seawater, and this tale is not an old one, but then again, maybe it is. After all, there was the business of the water sprite, and water sprites aren't just old, they are ancient.

Our Annabelle Lee was a young cocker spaniel of unknown lineage. Saved from some awful fate as a pup. You would have thought she could be just a tad more grateful for her improved status in life. As it was, she always had her eyes locked on the horizon, while she paced and worried about some unseen what-if that lay just on the other side of the fence. It wasn't just the other side of the fence, but also the other side of the door, the other side of the window, and even sometimes the other side of the room. Poor Annabelle Lee was so busy worrying about all the things she couldn't see, things that might be there, things that might try to do something to her, that truthfully, about the best you could say for her was she was trying to find

28

her courage. It wasn't that she lacked courage, it was just that she couldn't find where she had stored hers most of the time.

Annabelle came to me twice a week. One day she came all by herself and a few days later she would come back with her owners. The plan was to teach Annabelle how to be successful with enough different things to give her confidence. With her growing confidence she would stop misplacing her courage.

The entire program was really working well for her, and slowly she was developing more and more confidence in her own abilities and this made it possible for her to remember where she was keeping her courage.

This story is not about how Annabelle spent her days in doggie day care or training, but about how she finally found the courage to deal with the water sprite.

"Water sprite?" you ask

"Water sprite," I answer.

No question about it. There simply had to be a water sprite living in the back part of the automatic water bowl.

For those of you who are unfamiliar with all things doggie, an automatic water bowl is self-filling. It is attached to a garden hose and the water is then turned on. A float valve in the covered back compartment monitors the water level and automatically allows more water into the bowl as the dog drinks.

The hissing sound and the water bubbling into the bowl normally doesn't bother the dogs. Then again, most dogs understand the float has to be controlled by someone. Who better qualified than a wandering water sprite?

In case you are wondering, water sprites can be rather benign sorts; happy to mind their own business, do the job they were assigned, and most of the time they behave. Beware the human who angers a water sprite, because when angry they are quite able to do truly awesome damage. Have you ever seen, just as a for instance, what happens when the ruling water sprite in a mild, gentle, playful creek gets angry? I have. Why, I saw that sprite rear up, snarling and growling, pick up a full sized car, and toss it almost a half mile down stream, and then just leave it there. So I found myself in complete sympathy with Annabelle's worries.

This particular lesson day was hot and humid. The work was causing everyone problems and the 'you have to get it right before you quit' rule was especially difficult on the three students. Finally, all three of them had been successful; the time to stop and take a break had come. None too soon as far as Annabelle was concerned. She had worked up a powerful thirst and headed straight for the water bowl as soon as she heard 'okay'. 'Okay' was her release word, the word that told her she was free to follow her own interests in a quiet ladylike manner.

All she was thinking about was how good that drink of water would be. Lap, lap, lap, lap, and then IT happened.

Annabelle had managed to drink enough water to lower the water level, and the water sprite did her job. She opened the valve and allowed more water to flow into the bowl. The water gurgled and chuckled, and the sprite hissed as she worked the valve. At that very instant Annabelle forgot where she had placed her courage.

"BARK!! Screech!! Help me, help, bark, me. That thing is going to get us all", Annabelle jumped back in total confusion. Not one single human moved. They all just stood there. The water sprite continued to do her work, totally ignoring Annabelle's cries.

Thirst drove Annabelle back to the bowl, and she ever so carefully extended her head toward the water. Slowly she stuck her tongue out and started to take another lap.

"Hiss. Bubble, bubble. Gurgle."

At once, Annabelle jumped way back, and with her tail clamped firmly between her legs, she began to bark hysterically.

This was more than Aviva, her owner, could bear. "Poor Anna. Oh poor Annabelle", she crooned, "don't worry, it won't hurt you."

I spoke up, "Hush. Leave her alone. Give her time to work this out."

Annabelle crept slowly back towards the noisy, spitting water bowl. She really wanted to be able to finish her drink, and she knew she had to find out what was causing the bowl to hiss and bubble at her. The effort of returning was enormous. Annabelle shook and quivered. She crouched down on her belly and slowly slid closer and closer, stopping every so often to reach into her courage place and grab just a little bit.

Finally, she was close enough to reach the water. This time she decided she would just bite the darn thing first, and then get her drink. Quickly she shot her head forward and bit the side of the bowl just as hard as she could.

"Hiss, sssss, blurb", Annabelle let out a scream and literally flew backwards.

"Oh you poor, poor, poor baby" and Aviva stepped up to the bowl and started to splash the water.

At the same time, I literally barked at Aviva to get back and mind her own business or she would have to go sit in the car. Then Levi, Aviva's husband, started laughing really hard. Annabelle knew that even if nothing else happened, she had to find her courage just to protect Aviva. Someone was going to have to take on the job, and there were two humans present who didn't seem to care about all the danger.

With this thought firmly held in her mind, Annabelle once again began her approach. The closer she got, the more determined she became. With head down, tail tucked tightly between her legs and body all aquiver, Annabelle inched herself close enough to touch the side of the bowl. This time, she was going to be much smarter. This time it wouldn't be able to do a single thing to her. She paused. She gathered up all her strength and actually found some of her missing courage.

Bap! Slap! Bap! Slap! Using her front paws, she hit that water bowl. A quick left, right followed by a second left, right. Wonder of wonders, the bowl sailed backward across the pavement for about two feet. Almost all the water sloshed out, and the water sprite was called in to open the float valve all the way. Water poured in, the hissing went on and on, and the bubbles almost seemed to jump out of the water. Not a single bubble was able to reach Annabelle.

Having now located the place where all her courage was stored, Annabelle walked up and sniffed. Yes, it was true those bubbles were all but jumping out of the bowl. And yes, it was true the sprite was hissing at a furious rate. But that was all that was happening. The sprite couldn't seem to actually come after her. So Annabelle lowered her head, stuck out her tongue and drank her fill.

Finishing her drink, she became aware of the fact that the humans were all laughing. Hum... that was well worth looking into. And with that thought, Annabelle took her paw and slapped the side of the bowl hard. Lots of water sloshed out. The humans chuckled. So Annabelle took her nose and started shoving the thing around on the pavement. More and more water sloshed out and the water sprite had to work at a frantic pace to keep up.

With the sprite working so hard, the hissing sound was especially loud and insistent. Judging by the sounds of laughter coming from all three humans, Annabelle figured she was doing alright and this gave her a chance to locate even more courage.

She pounced. Both front feet landed firmly in the bowl. By now, Annabelle was no longer quivering. Her tail, rather than being clamped between her legs was up in the air and wagging wildly. This was actually fun. Bark, bark, bark, the humans just continued to laugh, not one of them told her to stop barking.

Annabelle stepped back to catch her breath. This was fun. She couldn't imagine why she had been so worried in the beginning. It was now quite clear to her that the water sprite couldn't leave the bowl. Annabelle ran around and around in a tight circle, barking and pretending to lunge in and bite. Hiss, hiss, hiss was all she got for her trouble.

Finally, she reached the conclusion that she would just have to be more forceful and make that water sprite come out and show herself. With that thought in mind, Annabelle lunged in, slammed both front paws in the bowl and took a big bite at the back compartment. For all her effort the only things that happened were lots of water splashed and sloshed out of the bowl, and the humans laughed even harder.

Fun, fun, fun and Annabelle started digging in the bowl as fast as she could. Water flew everywhere. The water sprite hissed and hissed. Oh, glorious day! Today, Annabelle remembered where she was storing her courage, and she had a wonderful time.

You know, one can never tell about things. With enough education, Annabelle Lee just might learn to love and be loved. She certainly is on her way, now that she has found where her courage is stored.

Footnote: This story was written for Jason, Yael and their young Annabelle Lee. Just hang in there. MW

"The Devil finds work for idle hands."
Proverb. *(1721)*

Come To Me

Poke, poke, poke. "Go away, I mean it!"

Poke. "G O   A W A Y."

Five minutes later: Poke, poke, poke. JAB! "True, go away and let me sleep."

Less than a minute later: Lick, lick. Poke. Jab. Lick. "True, if you don't let me sleep, I am going to get really mad. Now, go away!"

"Sigh." With that, True threw herself down on the floor, and glared at Girl. "Stupid, you are really going to make the Boss mad if you keep up with what you are doing."

"Ha! Just because you are an Imperial Walker doesn't make you always right. Besides, you are just jealous 'cause I found them first." With that, Girl went back to her chewing.

True watched Girl and her chewing for several more minutes and then nudged Justice. Justice mumbled something under her breath and went over to Girl. Giving a classic Doberman ugly face, Justice took the sandal away from Girl, dropped it next to where the Boss was sleeping and went back to her spot by the door.

For a while there was quiet. Quiet can be boring when you want to do something, anything but just lying around doing nothing. Girl started to fidget. She reached out with a paw and pulled one of the big hard bones to her and started to gnaw on it. It was not interesting. All the good stuff had

34

long since been sucked and licked out of the middle, and the outside part was tasteless. Giving up on that bone, Girl next tried to chew on one of the softer nylabones piled in a corner of the hallway. Chew bones were not what she wanted either as she eyed the sandal again.

No one moved. The Boss continued to sleep on the sofa. Justice and True both had their eyes closed and didn't seem the least bit interested in what Girl was starting to do. So Girl moved a little closer to the sandal. True stirred. Girl froze.

A couple of minutes passed and no movement or even a sigh came from any of the three sleepers. Girl inched closer to the sandal and carefully extending a paw, she snagged it. Just as her paw got a good grip on the sandal strap, True opened her eyes and stared straight at Girl. With her top lip starting to lift in the beginning of an ugly face, True continued to stare at Girl.

Girl slowly withdrew her paw and started to whine. "Come on, True, what difference does it make? Just let me have a few more good chews, please."

True stood and stretched. She walked over to the sandal, calmly picked it up in her mouth, and moved it under the Boss' desk.

"Listen up, brat. You don't seem to understand much of anything. This kind of chewing makes the Boss turn into a fire-spitting monster. You really don't want to know just how awful that can be when it is turned on you."

Still whining, Girl turned her back on True. "You just wait, one of these days I'm going to be an Imperial Walker just like you. Then you won't be able to order me around."

"Get a grip, bonehead, YOU will never be an Imperial Walker. Only properly schooled Dobermans can be Imperial Walkers. You are too short. You are the wrong color and you don't understand a thing about guard duty. Why don't you just to learn how to carry a duck or something?"

Girl didn't even bother to look at True. She just lay there with her back turned and her head resting on her paws. The problem with this new position was that she now faced the room that held the other sandal. The room with the sandal just kept beckoning and calling. Little soft whispered calls. Not one single other dog seemed to be able to hear these whispered words of enticement. Girl just knew the lone sandal was calling to her. She wiggled around a bit and then rolled over. This put her not only in the hallway, but also just beyond the doorway to the office.

She didn't move a muscle for the longest time, and then again came the whispered temptation. "Come to me, come to me." Girl was sure that was what she was hearing. Slowly, ever so slowly, she stood and on silent feet padded into the bathroom. Sure enough, there lay the lone sandal just begging her to pick it up.

Girl lay down and closed her eyes. She figured if she didn't look at it, she wouldn't be tempted to start chewing. Her mouth started watering. Soon the drool was forming long strings of saliva at the corners of her mouth. She twitched and licked her lips and, unable to stand it any longer, she lifted her head and chomped on the sandal.

Girl began to chew on the sandal in earnest. After a time when no fire-spitting monster burst into the room, she started to relax. Not liking to be alone when everyone else was in another room, Girl, carrying the sandal in her mouth, quietly returned to her place in the doorway to the office. After she got comfortable, she realized that everyone continued to sleep which just naturally meant Girl was free to chew. Chew she did, spitting out the little pieces that sometimes came loose. Every once in a while, she would bite off a piece, chew for a while and then swallow. There was less and less of the sandal with each passing minute. Girl was actually eating the Boss' sandal.

Time passed, and finally True opened her eyes just in time to see Girl take another bite of the sandal between her paws. True's eyes got wide, very wide indeed. Without meaning to, one of True's back legs kicked out and slammed Justice right in the side. This woke Justice up with a start. Waking Justice up suddenly like that was never a good idea, and this time was no exception. Since Girl was the very first thing Justice saw, it was toward Girl that the ugly face, ugly words, and a hard pinch were directed. Girl let out a squeal and dropped what was left of the sandal. Justice let out a roar when she saw that the dropped sandal was the second sandal to be chewed.

Meanwhile, True had gone back to poking and licking the Boss to wake her up. This time it worked, and the Boss uncovered her eyes, gave True a pat and sat up. It took a minute before anything happened. Justice and True used that time to slowly back out the other office door.

When the explosion came, they were both already on the porch, and it took only a quick second for them to be down the ramp and into the yard. Their rapid exit left Girl to find out about fire-spitting monsters all on her own.

Girl couldn't believe her eyes. The Boss seemed to be at least as tall as the ceiling and was waving her arms around and screaming. Girl couldn't understand a single word being said, but she sure could tell by the odor coming from the Boss that she was truly furious. Girl had never seen anyone behave like this.

She just continued to wave her arms and yell about her sandal until she saw the other sandal, which happened to be the point when Girl realized that both Imperial Walkers were gone. They had left her all alone to face the towering rage that did indeed seem to be spitting fire. Still screaming and now hitting the remains of one sandal against the other partially eaten sandal, the Boss slowly turned toward Girl.

'*WHO.*"

"*DID.*"

"*THIS.*"

"*TO.*"

"*MY.*"

"*SANDALS?*"

As the words rolled out of the Boss' mouth, Girl was sure she could see the flames wrapping around each and every sound.

Making herself as small and insignificant as she was able, Girl crept carefully past the Boss and slipped out the door into the yard. Once in the yard, Girl ran as fast as she could toward the back fence and a place to hide. She could still hear the monster screaming and roaring behind her. After a time, things went back to quiet in the house, Justice and True could be seen coming and going through the office doorway in a normal, everyday sort of way. Girl figured it would be safe for her to come out of hiding and pretend she didn't know there had been anything wrong.

When it came time for dinner, the Boss called everyone in the house just like always. The only thing that was different was that funny smell was still clinging to the Boss, and Girl felt eyes burning a hole in the back of her head. Girl ducked her head and hurried to get into the kennel where she would eat her dinner. Both Justice and True totally ignored her; sometimes they could be so mean.

At least nothing more was said about the sandals that had become an afternoon snack. Girl figured the storm had pretty much blown over, and she didn't have to worry about it any more.

Day followed night, and Girl noticed the funny smell was no longer clinging to the Boss. She relaxed and memories of the fire-spitting monster faded into the hazy past. After dinner each evening, everyone lounged around in the office while the Boss worked on the computer. As usual, Girl was bored. She got to thinking about the lovely chew she had enjoyed a few days before. Then she decided she wasn't at all comfortable where she was and headed for the bathroom to stretch out on the floor.

Throwing herself down on the bathroom floor, Girl heaved a huge sigh and closed her eyes. She wiggled and twisted looking for a comfortable position and as she moved a scent drifted by. "Sniff. Sniff. Sniff." Girl opened her eyes and looked around for the location of the lovely smell.

Eyes widening, mouth starting to water, Girl spotted a pair of old leather moccasins lying on the floor only a few feet from her nose. Not even bothering to consider that the smell was just the same as the smell of the sandals from a few days before, Girl stood up and with a couple of quick steps had one of the moccasins in her mouth. That moccasin felt good in her mouth, but even better, it tasted wonderful. Carrying the moccasin in her mouth, Girl returned to her place in the office doorway. She flopped down and began to chew slowly and gently on the moccasin.

True opened her eyes and stared at Girl in total disbelief. Surely after what had happened a few days ago, Girl wouldn't be foolish enough to chew up another of the Boss' shoes? After watching for a couple of minutes, True got up and not saying a single word to Girl began to poke the Boss with her nose.

The Boss patted True on the head and continued to peck away at the keyboard. True poked harder and the Boss stopped what she was doing and turned to look at True. "What do…?" she started to say. Then her eyes fell on Girl.

True, seeing that she had accomplished what she set out to do, quickly got out of the way. Giving Justice a swift pinch as she headed out the door, True was gone in a blink.

Justice came awake with a jerk, an ugly face in the making and a snarl in her throat. She took one look at Girl, the moccasin and the Boss. One look was all that was necessary and Justice too, was gone in the twinkling of an eye.

Meanwhile, the Boss had totally disappeared. Where the Boss had been sitting the fire-spitting monster rose and towering over Girl roared, '*WHAT*"

"*ARE*"

"*YOU*"

"*DOING?*"

Girl cringed, dropped the moccasin and tried to run. The monster's hand came out of nowhere to stop her dead in her tracks.

Girl couldn't move. The rage and the fury rolled over her in waves. The smell coming from the monster was awful. All Girl could do was squeeze her eyes tight shut and whimper. For a second there was quiet while the monster took another breath. Girl opened one eye. The roaring started up again and now the monster was waving the moccasin under her nose. Girl tried to turn her head away. The monster wouldn't let her. More roaring, and then it got awful still. Girl opened her eyes. The monster stood there staring at her through hot, fire-rimmed eyes. There was the smell of fire in the air. At least, that was what Girl thought the smell might be.

In fiery words she could almost see, Girl heard the monster order her to a kennel. On her belly, Girl headed toward the room where there was a kennel, once there she crawled into it and squeezed her eyes tight shut. She heard and felt the door being slammed behind her. The next morning when the Boss came to let Girl out of the kennel, she came out very carefully and keeping an eye out for the monster hurried outside.

"Morning, punk", True nipped Girl on the shoulder as she came into the yard. "So tell me, have you learned anything at all?"

"Where does that fire monster come from?"

Justice walked up at that point, and hearing the question, said, "None of the dogs know where the monster comes from, and none of us know where it goes. What we do know is that you don't want to do anything to open the door and set it loose."

True joined in, "The other thing we know is that sometimes when the monster gets loose all the dogs suffer."

"Is that the reason you poked the Boss and told on me?"

"Of course not." True was starting to get tired of the entire conversation. "I am an Imperial Walker, and it is my duty to keep the Boss informed of all things that are out of order."

"Stop breaking the laws," Justice said over her shoulder, and both she and True headed to a section of the fence in need of their attention. There was a strange human on the other side and he might be foolish enough to come too close.

Girl didn't even bother to try and follow them; she just went to the water dish and started digging all the water out onto the pavement. At least she knew she wasn't going to accidentally call the monster that way, and the water sprite was fun to annoy. Just a little while later the gate opened and Whim joined the group. Girl's day was starting to look better and better while memories of the monster faded into the background.

"Friendship often ends in love; but love in friendship – never."
Charles C. Colton

Hot Night at the Regency

June Dalton had a problem and I was her solution. At least that is what the message on my answering machine said.

"Hello? May I speak to June Dalton?"

"This is June."

"Hi June. I'm calling from All Good Dogs. You called and left a message about a problem with a dog?"

"Thank goodness you called back. I've got an awful problem. Last night I was coming in pretty late and a car roared passed me, slowed down a little bit, tossed this puppy out the door, then sped back up and disappeared around the corner. What am I going to do?"

"Back up a little and give me some more information. First, where do you live?"

"I'm living in a condo in Brookville and I don't even know if they allow dogs. This is just a puppy, how could someone?"

"Oh there are people out there who are less than good, kind or honorable and I think you just received the work of one of them. Why don't you bring the pup over here this afternoon after you get home from work and at least let me take a look? Who knows? Maybe I can come up with an idea for you."

It was about 6:30 p.m. that evening when June showed up. The pup was female, about 25 rather skinny pounds and looked to be about 4 months of

41

age, give or take a week or two. She had a short thick coat, prick ears and a long bushy tail. This pup was of very undeterminable ancestry with two rather unusual characteristics and a really great temperament. First she was carrying double dewclaws on both of her hind legs and second she was a brindle coloration that followed the most distinct tiger striping pattern I have ever seen on a dog.

"Well, since she is definitely a mixed breed pup I think we can rule out her having been stolen from some place. Her mixed breed status also rules out my being able to contact a breed rescue group or a breed specialty club to see if we could locate an owner or breeder. So this means your choices are to turn her over to animal control, keep her and train her or take her to a vet and have her killed. Considering her size and probable age, plus the fact she is a mixed breed means a trip to the animal control shelter will also likely mean death. Then again, she will at least have a chance at a home."

"Kill her? Kill her? That's awful. I could never"

I cut her off by asking, "Have you checked to find out what the condo rules are about dogs?"

"Yes. No dogs allowed."

"Well, it looks as if the only thing to decide is whether it will be animal control or the vet."

"No way! She is much, too much of a love and I'm keeping her. Since I'm renting and my lease is almost up, I'll just keep her hidden until I can find us another place to live. Besides which, I really hate living alone."

"Good for you. Okay then, here is what I suggest. First, let's get her enrolled in the next novice class. It still has a couple of openings and is due to start next Wednesday evening. Next let's sign her up for day care Monday through Friday. You can drop her off on your way to work and pick her up on the way home. That way she won't be around during the day when you aren't there and she will get enough exercise so you won't have to worry about where you are going to take her to exercise after you get home in the evening. Tomorrow you need to take her to see a vet and get her checked out and started on her shots. How is that for a plan?"

"I like it. Let me fill out the registration for class and day care right now. What should I feed her? And I can't keep carrying her every where, so what should I use to walk her?"

So it went and by the time June left with her pup she had a name; a collar; a six-foot, leather leash; a fifteen foot longe line plus the name of the brand of food to feed and a catalogue so she could order a kennel and all sorts of other puppy goodies. The pup's name? Love. In fact on the application for class she wrote the name as "Such a Love". Cute, huh?

Love started in day care two days later and when Wednesday rolled around she started her obedience training. Sometimes I think there is much to be said for the idea that pups live up to the names we give them. This little gal was quick and eager to learn and just seemed to fit right in, no matter where you put her. She was sure living up to her name.

The week after June and Love started their classes a new class started on Tuesday evening. I don't always get to see all the dogs until that first night, so I was totally unprepared to meet Grant and Secret. Sometimes there will be a dog or a person, usually dog, that just jumps right out at me when I first walk into the training area on a first night. Yeah I know, bet you think when I say, "jumps right out at me" I mean that the dog lunges at me. Nope, that is not what I mean. I mean there is something about the dog that just makes it stand out from all the rest. This was the case with Secret, since the application had stated the breed as Tasmanian Trufflehound and I was pretty sure that was a joke.

Secret was a slightly larger version of Love. Right down to the double dewclaws on the hind legs, Secret looked just like Love. Same brindled tiger stripe markings, same short, dense coat, and same prick ears. He even looked to be about the same age. During the break that is always scheduled as a part the first class, I walked over to Grant and asked him to please stay after class because I wanted to talk to him about Secret.

When class was over, talk we did. It turned out that Grant lived on the other side of town from June. He had a small home in Milestone Manor. This was a very upscale, new development of lovely homes and it seemed strange to see him with a dog that looked so much like a pup that had been dumped from a moving car.

"I was out walking pretty late one evening a couple of weeks ago. When the weather is nice I like to take a before bed stroll around the lake. I was just coming around the far end, down where the boat rental and dock are when a beat-up old jalopy of a car came roaring passed. They slowed down just enough to toss a pup out the window and then sped off. I thought the pup was dead and went to check. Turned out he wasn't quite dead, so I carried him home and then to the vet and then decided to keep him. Just couldn't turn such a fighter away."

"I can certainly understand your feelings. So tell me, why the name and where did you come up with the breed?"

"Well, it was just chance that I happened to take a walk that evening. It had been raining almost all day. It was just chance that I happened to be by the dock when the car went by and someone tossed him out the window. In my neighborhood no one has a mixed breed and I decided it would be fun to be the owner of a very rare breed. By the time I got him home from the vet he had become a rare Tasmanian Trufflehound named Secret Chance."

I just shook my head as Grant continued, "See what his breed really is will always be a secret and I took a chance on taking him in."

"Grant, I really like you. Like your sense of humor, your willingness to go a little extra for a dog. Now, I have a request to make. Would you please bring Secret back tomorrow evening? Try to be here about 8 p.m. There is someone the two of you simply must meet."

Unfortunately it was a full month before Grant's schedule and June's schedule finally made it possible for them to meet up after one of Grant's classes. It was really too, too funny to watch the expressions on both their faces as they looked at the other's dog. Tell you the truth; I suspect my face didn't look much different. The two dogs really did look alike. There could be no doubt at all that whatever their background had been, one thing was sure, they really were from the same litter of pups. June liked Grant's idea for a breed name and from that point forward Love stopped being a mixed breed and become a rare Tasmanian Trufflehound.

Both owners finished their respective classes and both went on to the next level of training. By that time they were training together several times during each week, dating and just in general enjoying each other and both the dogs. Between them they cooked up this rather outrageous story about the dogs. How the breed was almost extinct, how this pair had been smuggled out of the jungle in carry sacks and flown by private jet back to this country. It seemed as time went on the story just took on a life of its own.

There was another thing that was taking on a life of its own. That was a budding romance between Grant and June. By the time summer was coming to a close it was apparent to everyone who knew them that they were getting serious about way more than Secret and Love. Off and on starting in late fall and all through the winter months I would get Secret and Love as boarders while Grant and June went off for a weekend of color watching. They headed first to Massachusetts and then to Pennsylvania and finally to a hide-away in the Shenandoah Valley to watch the leaves change color. Or so they said to anyone who happened to ask, "why all the traveling?" Then right after the holidays were over came a couple of trips to a ski resort. Next they headed off to the Cayman Islands and by now there was no question in anyone's mind as to what was going on. The big question was when was there going to be a wedding?

When they returned from the Cayman's June told me they had made the big decision and the wedding would be in September. She said that since neither she nor Grant had much family and they both had come to think of everyone they knew at All Good Dogs as family, did I think it would be okay if they invited everyone to the wedding? Just as soon as she had the details worked out and a firm date would it be possible to book Secret and Love to stay with me while they were on their honeymoon?

I can't say I was surprised about the wedding. I was totally amazed by the invitation. The idea that I could now add matchmaker to my resume really amused me and I was delighted to be keeping Secret and Love because of a honeymoon. Things were definitely looking good for all four of them.

But there was no way that was going to continue and sure enough the first bump in the road wasn't long in coming. Someone finally realized that June had an illegal houseguest. Namely one very rare breed Tasmanian Trufflehound named Love. June was told she had 15 days to either get rid of Love or get out. Of course, I couldn't understand why she didn't just go ahead and move in with Grant. But I'm not much of one for standing on ceremony if said ceremony was going to get in the way of being practical.

June felt otherwise. So she stayed put and Love moved in with Grant and Secret. The one thing I did manage to talk her into doing was to continue to keep Love in day care at least for the time being. And that was how I ended up with both dogs in day care. Grant had never given the idea of day care for Secret much thought until he saw how much Love enjoyed it.

There were more and more bumps as the time got closer and closer to the actual wedding date. I really can see lots of reasons why some couples vote to just slip off and have a very quiet ceremony and then come back and announce the marriage as a done deal. There were problems with where the reception was going to be held. There were problems with the caterer. The place they wanted to go on their honeymoon didn't have any room. On and on went the list to the point where I was beginning to wonder if this wedding would actually take place at all. As for the two dogs, if they hadn't been in day care I think they would have been totally forgotten. June became more and more frantic in her arrangements, while Grant grew surprisingly cool and almost remote.

There was one really stormy morning when June seemed particularly tense. I made the mistake of asking her what was wrong and she just burst into tears. There was no place for them to go on the honeymoon. Every single place they had agreed on was already booked and her best friend wasn't speaking to her because of the color of the bridesmaids' dresses and the flowers were too expensive and Grant wasn't any help and, well you get the picture.

So that afternoon when he stopped by to pick up both the dogs, I suggested that Grant offer to take over making all the arrangements for the honeymoon. That he tell June where they would be going would be a surprise and that she should not worry about that part of the planning any more.

He took my advice and much to my amazement, June was delighted to hand that job over to him. He turned right around and hit me up for suggestions.

"Where to go? You want me to find a place for you to go on your honeymoon? Grant, honey, I'm just a dog trainer. Why me? Why not a travel agent? Why not your Mom? Shoot why not ask Secret for a suggestion."

Oh no, it had to be me since I was the one who introduced them and it had been my idea that he offer to handle all the arrangements for the travel and the honeymoon. Actually I did have an idea, something just a little different from the sort of thing they normally did. In fact, it wasn't even in the general direction they normally traveled. Either it would be a great idea or it would totally bomb out.

"Grant, have you ever been to Victoria? You know, the Victoria that is in British Columbia? I was there a couple of years ago for a conference. It is really nice and while I was there I got to see this really great old hotel. It's right in the heart of the original downtown business district. Its historic, romantic and just the place to spend a honeymoon and in this case historic is not being used as a euphemism to cover up old and run-down."

"Never been to the Pacific Northwest and I don't think June has either. What's this place like?"

"Well, keep in mind that I only saw a small part of it and I'm two years out of date. The room I saw was really impressive. Sort of narrow, but it had a big window complete with window seat that looked out over the Inner Harbor. That room had a working wood burning fireplace, a whirlpool tub and a featherbed on the queen-sized bed. There was also a lounge complete with a live jazz band on Saturdays and a snooker table. Anyway, the name of the place is the Bedford Regency and it just might be the answer to the honeymoon dilemma.

The long and the short of it was that the Bedford Regency was the place. They ended up spending two weeks there. June told me that what with the fire in the fireplace and the view of the harbor and well just everything that there was more than one hot night. We had a lot of fun teasing them about a hot night at the Regency caused by the chance encounter of Secret Love.

There are dogs that herd, dogs that hunt, dogs that retrieve, dogs that are companions and then there are the dogs that are matchmakers. Isn't it amazing the number of things a good dog or two manages?

"Whenever you are asked if you can do a job, tell 'em, 'Certainly I can!' Then get busy and find out how to do it."
Theodore Roosevelt (1858-1919)

Rags and the Italian Shoes

I have always thought the color red really did a lot to brighten up a gray outfit. The soft leather shoes were a lovely shade of red and I'm sure would have gone really well with the dark gray pants suit Fionna was wearing. Actually, what was left of the shoes looked good next to Rags, since he was a Bearded Collie and the red made a nice contrast to his gray and white shaggy coat.

"My beautiful shoes! I paid four hundred dollars for these shoes and now look at them. For years I dreamed of owning a pair of real Italian shoes, and now all I have left are a few chewed pieces." With that, Fionna started to cry.

"*Four hundred dollars for a pair of shoes?*" I'm thinking to myself. Now I will grant they did look like really comfortable shoes. At least at one time I'm sure they were really comfortable. The leather was that soft, supple sort of leather that just begs to be right next to your skin. And the color - oh the color! A shade of red that just made the day seem a little brighter. Unfortunately, the left shoe was missing the entire heel and a chunk from the toe; the right shoe was missing the entire toe. In their present condition they were past the uncomfortable to wear stage. Now they were totally unwearable and sadly way past repairable. Rags had really done a number on them.

"Well, you can teach him to leave your shoes alone. That would be one place to start; however, it sure won't get this pair back for you. The major problem with teaching him to leave your <u>shoes</u> alone is that he will then just turn to chewing up something else. You won't be happy about that either."

"What am I supposed to do?" Fionna actually wailed her question.

"My suggestion would be to get really busy and start training Rags with an eye toward giving him some real jobs. After all, Beardies are known for their high energy levels. If you don't give him something to do, then he will find something; and you don't really want to know what the next something will be."

Fionna had called me the week before to set up an appointment for Rags because Sean, Fionna's boyfriend had warned her she was going to have to do something, or else. I didn't ask, and Fionna didn't elaborate on just what that 'or else' would be. She evidently had some ideas though, because the warning had been enough to spark her calling me. Then last night while she and Sean were out for the evening, Rags had gotten hold of her wonderful shoes. The ensuing damage to those shoes meant she wasn't really in the best frame of mind to start training.

The long down is one of those exercises that is truly elegant in simplicity. All the human needs is a metal folding chair, a flat leash (preferably leather), a snug fitting collar, and of course the required recalcitrant rover. With the dog on the left side and the leash stretched across the seat of the chair, allowing the dog only just enough slack to stand, sit or lie down, all the owner needs do is just to sit there. Having assigned her the task of sitting on Rags, which was my way of saying she was making it possible for him to learn a long down and patience all at the same time, I started asking questions.

"How long have you had Rags?"

"He's two years old now, and I got him as a puppy."

"Have you done any sort of training with him at all? I mean training other than housebreaking and walking on a leash."

"Well, he is housebroken, but I'm not so sure about walking on a leash. He pulls so hard and jumps around so much that it is much easier to just put him out in the backyard."

"Okay, so you don't walk him very much. Does he come when you call him?"

"Sure he does. Except when there are squirrels in the trees, or the kids next door are playing ball, or the dog that lives behind us is out, or the UPS truck is going down the street."

"So tell me what sort of things do you do with Rags?"

"Do with Rags? I brush him. I feed him. I let him in and out. What else would I do with a dog?"

That was just the sort of answer that made my teeth curl. No wonder Rags had eaten her fancy Italian shoes! Here was yet another person who didn't have a clue - not a clue! - and the poor dog was the loser. Well, not quite a total loser. He had eaten her red shoes, and he was here, so all was most definitely not lost.

"Tell you what I want you to do. I want you to spend the next six weeks working on his training, and then let's plan to sit down again and talk about what you want to do with Rags. How is that?"

"Six weeks? I don't know if…" she never finished the sentence because Rags picked up what was left of one of the red shoes. Just that quickly he was signed up for lessons.

The first week of training had gone very well for both Fionna and Rags. When they showed up for their second lesson, Rags was much calmer. Of course, calm is a relative term. Rags was calmer than he had been the week before, but if you were in the market for a slow, sedentary sort of dog, you would have to look elsewhere. What was of even more interest to me was that Fionna was also much calmer and definitely not as jerky in her movements as she had been when I first saw her. To me this change said she had really spent some time working with Rags and the work was as good for her as it was for him.

"Watching you and Rags coming across the parking lot and through the gate, I know we can start right in on today's lesson. You really did your homework last week. So how do you feel about the ecollar now that you have had a chance to use it for a week?"

"I love this new collar! For the first time ever Rags is actually listening to me, and I don't have to scream or throw food at him."

I just love watching the wonderful change the ecollar brings about once my students get the hang of using it. In Fionna's case, it would seem that having to look at what was left of those red shoes of hers was enough of an incentive to really work hard with Rags.

"Now Fionna I want you to watch what I am going to show you, and then I will want you to try the same thing." So saying, I took Rags' leash and had him come to me a couple of times just to make sure he was ready to pay attention to what I wanted him to learn.

With the remote in my right hand and Rags' leash in my left hand, I told Rags to sit. At the very same time I said the word sit, I pulled up very gently on the leash and tapped the button on the remote. Well, actually I did a tap, tap, tap on the button. Rags sat. That was good. Unfortunately, before I could manage even the 'good' part of 'good boy' he had popped right back up. So I repeated the entire sequence. Again he sat and then popped up. Three more times I repeated the entire sequence and on the final try, Rags sat at once and stayed seated. I didn't even have a chance to move my right hand, let alone add the gentle, guiding upward pull. Better yet, not only did Rags stay in the sit, he watched me with expectant eyes.

At least I think this Bearded Collie was watching me and I was guessing about the expectant part. All that long, grey, silver and white hair was obscuring his eyes. The long white hair hung down in a part that ran the length of his muzzle. His body had an alert look to it, the wiggling on either side of his head I took to be ear movement. Hard to tell about ears since all I could see was long white hair on one side of his head and long grey hair on the other. Between the two sides and more or less in the middle the hair appeared to be standing straight up. Now I've seen dogs sporting topknots before. This looked like no topknot I had ever seen. It just looked like hair so full of electricity it was standing on end and gently waving in the breeze. My only other clue to where his attention might be focused was his tail gently thumping the floor.

How much can you know about a dog that is so shaggy you can't even see his eyes or his ears? The important part was that instead of jumping around, he was calmly sitting there facing in my direction. I was able to figure out the direction thing since I continued to be able to see that large black button nose. First I praised him with a very soft and quiet 'good boy', then released him from the sit with a pretty upbeat 'OKAY', and turned to Fionna.

Her mouth was hanging partly open as she just continued to stare at the two of us. Rags reacted first. In his normal, over-exuberant manner he took two high bounds and landed in front of Fionna with his front feet planted firmly on her shoulders.

"Rags, come." With that I started tap, tap, tapping on the button. Rags dropped back to the ground and trotted back to me.

"Okay, Fionna, now it is your turn. Do you understand what I did? Think you can do it as long as I talk you through it? Any questions before you start?" I handed both the leash and the remote to her.

"I don't believe I just saw that! Rags never, and I do mean never, sits. He hates sitting."

"Well, that was <u>before</u> you started the training and this is <u>now</u>. Things change, and so do dogs and people. Now hold the leash folded up the way I showed you, and get your thumb on that button. Ready? Okay, sit him."

Fionna was so tentative the first couple of times that I had to step in and help her out. After that, she got the hang of it and for the next ten minutes she and Rags sort of flowed around the training area with her giving the sit command every so often and Rags sitting faster and faster. Soon he was starting to sit as soon as she said 'Rags'.

"Time for a break. I don't want you to work on any one thing for more than about 10 minutes, and even that's pushing things. Baby steps will get the job done much faster than trying to hurry. Right now I want you to tell Rags "OKAY", give him a good pat, remove the leash, and just leave him alone. He really needs a break, and he has earned a good one."

By the end of the lesson, Fionna had progressed to the place where she was giving Rags sit commands from as far away as 15 feet, and Rags was responding properly every single time. Calling a halt to the lesson, I had Fionna release Rags to hang out while I went over the coming week's assignment.

"Remember, for this week you are going to want to break your training sessions into parts. You will use one part to work on the distance sit. Don't try to jump ahead because the last thing you want to be practicing with this guy would be mistakes. He needs to be back-tied with the 15-foot longe line every single time you work on those distance sits in a new area or one that isn't fenced. Your goal will be to give that sit command when you are 30 feet away and have him sit at once without any walking toward you. This is a really important building block, so don't skip it."

"What do you mean I am supposed to back-tie Rags?"

Remember how we used the longe line to tie Rags to the fence so you could walk away before you told him to sit? That is called back-tying, and it's how you will teach him to sit at a distance from you."

"What am I supposed to do about the come and heel command?"

"Oops, guess I wasn't clear enough on that one. The come command is the command you are going to use only when you want Rags to come TO you. The heel command is the command you are going to use when you want Rags to come WITH you. Big difference in how Rags is going to see the two commands. When you are moving and you want Rags with you, say "heel". When you are standing still and you want Rags to come to you, then you will tell him "come". Any other questions?"

Five weeks later, Fionna and Rags, having finished the first of the formal class lessons, were back - this time with Sean in tow. They wanted to show off just a little bit, and we needed to talk about future plans for Rags. He still needed a job in a big way.

Fionna and Rags ran through all the exercises in a manner that would have made any new dog owner really strut. In fact, that was exactly what both Fionna and Rags were doing! The couple of times I could glance over to where Sean was sitting, I saw a guy with a really big grin on his face. After the team had finished showing off, we sat down and started talking about the sort of things that would work for Rags. A major part of the criteria for this new job was going to be that it had to be enjoyable for both Fionna and Rags.

Fionna wasn't much interested in spending more time in teaching Rags new commands. I figured that was okay, the interest on her part would come later. Right now, we had to come up with something for Rags. Round and round we went. Finally I ask her if she had ever considered doing Pet Therapy with Rags.

"Pet therapy?" Both she and Sean started laughing.

"That's what I said, Pet Therapy. I'll just bet it's not what you think it is. There is a group in this area that takes well-trained and friendly dogs to nursing homes for visits. That is the sort of therapy I was thinking about."

"Oh, you're right", she grinned. "I thought you meant putting him on a couch and asking him what his problems were. Or maybe it was the other way around and he was going to put me on the couch."

53

"I thought that was where you were going when the two of you started to laugh. Nope, I really was thinking about how good Rags would be as a visiting dog in a nursing home. He is steady now, not jumpy at all, and he loves people. You can sit him on a dime, and he will just about give you nine cents change. Let me give you the number to call to see about getting him started."

So she called and made an appointment to be interviewed. Turned out it was a calling for both of them, and they ended up becoming something of a local celebrity team. Of course, they also discovered a real need for lots more training, but then you knew I was going to say that, didn't you?

The red shoes? The beautiful red Italian shoes? Sean gave Fionna a new pair for her birthday. Rags doesn't have any interest in them, he has a much higher calling now.

"It is possible to fail in many ways…while to succeed is possible only in one way."
Aristotle

Behind Those Eyes

When I got home from the airport, I parked my van, got out and walked around toward the rear. Opening the side door, I pulled the small crate forward and unlocked the door. The little dog really didn't want to come out, but at the same time she was not unwilling to let me guide her out. This was to be my first look at her.

You would think that, after spending the better part of two years looking for a specific dog, I would have a better idea of what to expect, but I really didn't. What I did know was that she was the right breed, sex, size and age. I knew she was a dog that some people would consider a failure of sorts. After all she had refused to show in the breed ring. She hadn't shown much aptitude for the obedience ring or the agility ring, and she wanted no part of being a kennel dog. Then she topped things off by being way too demanding to be considered a good pet. Why on earth had I ever said yes to the idea of even considering her? As I guided her out of that kennel, I really had doubts about my sanity, to be taking such a chance on a dog with this sort of a history. I must be even crazier to be actually considering her as a service dog - much less a service dog to replace a great service dog that had just died.

Once I had her out and on the ground, her beauty just about took my breath away. Carrying her head just so, ears in that perfect semi-fold so favored by breeders and connoisseurs of the Shetland Sheepdog, this little gal just floated across my parking lot. The white-collar blaze around her neck a perfect counterpoint to the white tip on her tail. But, and it was a big but, she wouldn't look at me. I tried every trick I knew to get her to even glance my way - no dice. She just wouldn't look.

"Okay sweetie, I know your history, but you don't know mine. We have a month to decide if this is what you want to do with the rest of your life. I sure hope it is, and not just because you are a pretty piece of fluff. Any little dog with as many opinions as they tell me you have, well…" I let my voice trail off.

At that point a freight train roared past. Yes, like it or not, I live right next to the railroad tracks. As the train roared, rattled and rumbled down the tracks, I glanced back down at Pixie to realize, much to my dismay, that she was way too sound sensitive. This was going to make for problems, and a small voice in my head said, "forget it, pretty is as pretty does, send her back". But I didn't and this is her story.

"He's dying, and you just have to find me a replacement." So started the sort of phone conversation that always leaves me with a strong feeling of anxiety and a sick feeling in the pit of my stomach. The voice on the other end of the line quivered with emotion and fear. Just the very idea of having to face the loss of a dog who has spent nine or ten years working as, not just your helper but an extension of your very person is more than enough to cause distress. No matter how hard a person may try to accept it, when it comes, the actual loss can be almost overwhelming.

When you train dogs, including Service Dogs, for a living sooner or later you are going to receive a call like that. After the first time it happens you will learn to dread hearing those words. Not only that, but you will keep right on doing the things that trigger those phone calls because the good feelings far outweigh the bad ones.

The dying dog was already nine years old and had been working full time as a service dog for almost eight of those nine years. Little did we know at the time of the call that this dog was so tough and so determined to continue doing his job that he would battle cancer for the next two and a half years just to buy us the time to find and train his replacement.

During the first year, I found and then rejected several dogs. They were either too tall or too small, or they didn't like the work, or they didn't get along well with other dogs or, well, you get the picture. Finding just the right dog was always tough. The search area continued to widen until it covered the entire country. By the time Pixie showed up, I was really starting to get worried. Then, on top of all this, her first week was a rough one, and I came very close to hitting my panic button.

I considered turning Pixie around and sending her back to her breeder. She wasn't thrilled about all the noise and confusion at my house. She wasn't thrilled about the vast number of dogs of many different breeds and sizes that were always around. She didn't like the ever changing kaleidoscope of humans that came to my house on a daily basis, and she didn't like the food. So why didn't I send her back? It was those eyes. Those eyes of hers never stopped watching, and on the couple of occasions when I was able to get her to actually make eye contact with me, I caught a glimpse of something behind those eyes that told me she really was the one. There was much more to this little piece of fluff than what was on the surface.

"She's eating now and isn't as nervous as she was. Best of all, she now has a sponsor." This was one of the best phone calls I had gotten to make since I made the call to say I thought I had found a replacement for Delta.

"You're joking about the sponsor, aren't you?" The voice on the other end of that line was so, so, well heavy, and tired sounding.

"Of course not. Have you ever known me to joke about sponsors? The strangest part of all is that things are starting to happen just like they did with Delta. It is all coming together in a way that makes me positive she is the right dog."

"You mean True is helping Pixie? Just like Charity helped Delta?"

Charity had been my partner and service dog when Delta came for training. At the time, the idea of Delta ever making it as a service dog seemed pretty far-fetched. Delta was too small or too tall, depending on your perspective. He was sound sensitive, a failure in the breed ring, a failure as a pet, and he washed out as a hearing assist dog. So why did I bother? Because.

"It just started yesterday, so maybe it's wishful thinking on my part, but twice when a train went by, Pixie ran to True and stood next to her the entire time. I'm going to give Pixie one more week to settle in, and then I'll start working her. Will let you know then what happens."

I continued to watch, and stay out of the way and each day I saw more of the helpful behavior. At first it was only related to noises, any loud noise would send Pixie flying to True for support. Later in the week, I started to notice that True was running a sort of interference for Pixie where the other dogs were concerned. By the end of the week, Pixie would stand and watch True start to eat. Only after True had started eating would Pixie turn and head to the place where her own food bowl had been placed, and best of all, she was eating. The first corner had been successfully turned.

I needed to find out just where Pixie stood as far as her formal training was concerned because I was going to have to have a starting point. One of the reasons for looking for an adult dog rather than a puppy was so I could start the serious service dog training right away and only have to spend a small amount of time on what I think of as etiquette and manners stuff.

With that in mind, I started taking Pixie for a walk every single day. By the third day, I could see she was going to need some help. The training was there, but her concerns about every single strange thing coupled with her problem with sounds, and she was really having a tough time. So True started going on these walks with us. Pixie would startle or hang back for loud noises or things like the mailbox. True would simply turn her head and give Pixie such a look - I don't have words that will describe that look, other than to say it sure was powerful, because Pixie would shake herself and move up to stand beside True. It was times like that when I would get a glimpse of what was behind those eyes of hers. There was a different sort of courage and a will as strong as steel lurking there.

"Well, today is the day. I put the ecollar on her this morning, and, after I finish talking to you, we are going out to start the serious training. I will be so glad to get rid of the leash and that old collar."

"I wish I could be there. Are you sure she is ready to start real training? Maybe you should give her some more time."

"Listen, we have to make a decision by the end of the week. Do you realize she has been here for more than three weeks? I can't keep putting it off. Either she is the right one or she isn't. We have to know for everyone's sake. So today is the day."

"Please call me as soon as you finish with the training. I'm not going to be able to do a single thing until I hear from you."

"Will do. Actually, I went ahead and sort of started things while we were talking. I figure from her reaction she is probably going to be a level three most of the time. At least, that is what she is responding to right now. I'll call you back for sure."

Shortly after I hung up the phone, Pixie and I headed outside to start some serious training. The first order of business for me was to introduce Pixie to the ecollar, my favorite training tool. Since I knew Pixie already knew what come and sit meant I figured things would go pretty quickly.

As it turned out, I sort of made a mistake by starting out with the come command. In retrospect, I realize I should have started with sit. That's the trouble with always doing things in the same order and in the same way. You, or at least I, get into a rut and forget that sometimes it is necessary to think outside the nice safe box.

Ecollar, short for electronic collar in its current form is a pretty new dog-training tool. Some people see the letters "e l e c t r" and they never really get much further. It's the same with hearing, some hear "electr" and never get any further. It's really too bad because there is a whole universe of difference between the "electr I C" and "electr O N I C". The word that ends in "ic" is strong enough to run your computer or light up a light bulb. The word that ends in "onic" is so weak the best it can do is send a short pulse from your TV remote to your TV or be the impulse sent out by the special tool your chiropractor uses to relax your muscles.

Bet I can just hear you thinking, "if it is so weak then why use it as a training tool?"

My answer is, <u>because</u> <u>it</u> <u>works</u>. It means I don't have to pull or be pulled, and I don't have to resort to what I think of as bribery. I don't have to yell and I don't have to jump up and down doing back flips.

What I do have to do is be fair, consistent, make sure the collar has been turned on, and remember to push the button. Oh, and I have to remember to give soft words of praise for a job well done. Even the words of praise will slowly go away as the dog begins to find satisfaction in the actual doing of the job.

Back to Pixie and my goof. Pixie was already something of a clingy dog, meaning she really didn't like getting very far away from what she viewed as her person. Just in the short time she had been with me, she had decided I would do as her person - at least I would suffice until something better came along. The feeling I got from Pixie on a daily basis was that, more than anything else, she wanted a person of her own. Not a person she had to share with even one other dog, but a person of her very own. Since True made it very clear to all the resident and visiting dogs that I was already taken, Pixie had to deal with being a low second place, if that.

So what did I do that was so wrong? I took this already clingy dog out and start introducing the ecollar via the come command. It only took me about five minutes to judge the entire thing a dismal failure. I drifted away from Pixie once and waited for her to get interested in one of the other dogs. Then I called her and tapped the button twice. She shot straight up in the air and hit the ground running. She didn't stop or even slow down until she smacked headfirst into my legs. After that one time, I couldn't get away from her. I tried to get away for the next half-hour, but nothing doing. No way was Pixie going to let me get more than about 6 inches from her. I gave up, called it a bad job, and went back in the house. The one thing I didn't do was to let Pixie come back in the house with me right then. At least I could get something right.

"Well, I just came in from working her, no make that attempting to work her."

"Oh no, what happened? You sure don't sound happy."

"I'm not. I'm so stupid. I know better than to start with a come command on a dog like Pixie. So don't even ask me why I started that way."

"Okay, so I won't ask why, but if you don't tell me what happened I am going to be really mad."

"She came."

'That's it? All you have to say is, 'she came?' What sort of an answer is that supposed to be, other than stupid?"

"I just told you what happened. I called her. I tapped the button. She came. And she wouldn't leave me, no matter what after that first call. I could just kick myself."

"So what are you going to do about it?"

"For today, nothing. Not a darn thing. Tomorrow is another day, and tomorrow I will start working her on sit. I have to be able to get away from her. Oh, and by the way, I forgot to tell you she started sleeping on the pillow next to my head last night."

"She what? You've got to be kidding. And True allowed it?"

The next day and for several days thereafter, Pixie and I worked on the sit command. It didn't take Pixie long to figure out that slamming her butt into a sit turned off the annoyance coming from the ecollar. At about the same time she figured out how to control the effects of my tap, tap, tapping on the remote button, she also started to develop some real personality.

What I saw slowly emerging was exactly what I had thought I had seen hiding behind those eyes of hers. She still wasn't real comfortable about making direct eye contact with me, but we were even making progress on that front. And she continued to sleep on the pillow next to my head every night. It never occurred to me to question the position since True didn't seem to mind.

Where did True sleep? On the bed next to me, of course. Goodness, what a silly question.

By the time we were well into the second month of Pixie's training, she had mastered all the foundation commands, and we were on our way to working on the specialty stuff. One of the neatest things that had shown up so far was the fact that Pixie laughed. When she was pleased with herself and the job she was doing, she would laugh.

I mean it. Really laugh. How? She would pull her lips back and expose her teeth, and then she would clack her teeth together and make this sort of gurgling sound in her throat. I just fell in love with that laugh. It got to where I was always thinking about how I could structure her training just so I could hear her laugh. Now I ask you, who was really in charge of the training? Sure I dreamed up the exercises and worked with her to get them right, but she was the one giving out the rewards.

One of the best days was the first time her retrieve became something useful. She had seen True bring me my shoes every day for as long as she had been with me. Finally one morning I decided it was time to test her, and I sent her for my shoes.

Well, she headed for the shoes as soon as she heard the fetch command. But when she got there, she just stood and stared at them, then she looked at True, then she looked back at me. I repeated my fetch command and this time went tap, tap, tap on the button of the remote. The look she gave me was an awful, just an awful look. Then she turned and looked at True. I repeated the fetch again and the tap, tap, tap on the remote's button.

All at once Pixie just dove at one of the shoes, grabbed it and half drug, half carried it back to me. I told her 'thank you' and re-sent her for the second shoe. This time she only hesitated long enough to glance in True's direction, and I had time for one tap. Before I could get in a second tap, both Pixie and my shoe were on their way back.

It was when I took that second shoe and said, 'thank you' that she began to laugh.

Laugh and spin and jump. Shoot, she all but did back flips, she was so proud. So I had been right all along, this little bit of Sheltie fluff, this little Pixie really did have a serious something behind those eyes of hers, and she was on her way to a full time career as a mobility assist service dog.

"We're on our way. She's here to stay. When do you want to start learning to work with her? I don't think you are going to find her to be much different from Delta. And best of all you are going to just fall in love with her laugh."

> "Persuasion is often more effectual than force."
> **Aesop**

Short Fences

When someone wants to talk about short fences, what do you think of? Do you think of fences that are low enough you can step over them, or do you think of fences that for some reason don't go all the way to the end of the line? Everyone knows that if a fence is too short any self-respecting dog will jump it. Then again, that would be talking about the vertical short and that is not the short I find interesting.

It is the horizontal short that is really fascinating when you start talking about dogs and fences. Horizontal short, meaning the one section of fencing is not long enough to meet up with the corresponding cross fence, thereby leaving a break in the perimeter of said fencing. If the opening has always been there, then both dogs and humans tend to treat it as a sort of pass-thru or gate. However, if this gap is new, ah now that is a whole other story. And that is the story of Gengis and Kubla and the large kennel where I started my career in dogs.

There they were, really going at it. This was the loudest and most aggressive fence fight I had ever seen or heard. The two young males were screaming, lunging, and snarling. Long ropes of spit were being slung through the air to land in big splats on the ground. Kubla knew he was the better dog and meant to rule. Gengis knew Kubla was lower than dried cat vomit and in need of killing. Down and back they raced, only to turn and race back again, and all the while the snarling, screaming and lunging continued. As I got closer, I could actually hear the teeth clicking with each snap of the mouth.

These two males always fought when they were kenneled next to each other, but never could I remember them fighting the way they were fighting this morning. My brain was screaming there was something wrong with the entire picture, but it wasn't until I was almost all the way to the gate of the first kennel run that I realized what was wrong. The fence was missing! What fool had turned those two out without checking the fence line? The storm last night had been one of those furious summer storms with high gusts of wind and lots of lightning - just the sort of storm guaranteed to bring down a tree limb. In this case, the storm had brought down an entire tree. Not a young, small tree, but a large, old poplar tree had crashed and totally flattened a long section of the fence between the two runs.

I was trying to figure out just how I was going to get the two of them apart and into separate quarters with the least amount of damage. Not another person was within shouting distance, and I only had the single kennel noose I always carried with me. With no help close at hand I was taking my time and trying to work out just how I was going to handle the problem. Thank goodness I was taking my time, or I might have missed what was actually going on.

To keep the dogs from getting bored, one of the things I had instructions to do was to regularly rotate them. This meant I was moving dogs from kennel paddock to kennel paddock on a regular basis. There was a rotation schedule posted, and we followed a specific pattern for moving the dogs to their new quarters each month. None of the males were to be kenneled next to a female in season, and males were supposed to be kenneled next to someone they liked to chase. Of course, this meant that I was responsible for doing a hands on, physical check of each dog every single day.

The kennel rotation did a couple of things. First it gave each dog a new place to explore with new smells, a different view, and, most importantly, new neighbors. When you put two dogs side by side in an enclosed area with a fence between them, they will do one of two things. If they know each other, after an initial greeting, they will ignore each other and very soon go back to sleeping most of the time. However, if the two dogs like to chase each other, well the sparks will fly - meaning they will run that fence line for hours at a time, day after day, for at least a couple of weeks - getting some much needed exercise in the process.

On the day of what I still think of as the "Day Of The Not Fight", there was an entire section of fencing missing. Not just a small opening but at least 20 feet of a 30 foot long fence gone, flattened by the large poplar that had fallen during the storm of the previous night. Think about it for a minute. Here were two dogs who by all indications were always ready to kill each other, and there was nothing holding them back. They shouldn't have even been in the runs they were in. They were supposed to be back at the kennel building. They were supposed to be in line for some serious grooming. They were supposed to… but no matter where they were supposed to be; the fact was they were in what had been adjoining runs. Now, for all intents and purposes, these adjoining kennel paddocks had been turned into one big paddock with a short section of chain link fencing dividing part of it down the middle.

Back and forth the two of them charged, screaming, lunging, and then it dawned on me what was actually going on. These two oh so serious combatants never, but never crossed the line where the fence had been. As far as they were concerned the fence was still there. I just forgot to worry about how I was going to separate them. I forgot about what I was going to say to explain how they had gotten so chewed up in a fight. All I could do was stand there and watch.

The noise brought more of the kennel help and yet not a one of us seemed able to move towards those two dogs. All we could do was stand there, frozen in place watching the most amazing "not fight" I had ever seen. To this day I still have never seen anything quite like it. Finally, both dogs as if by some hidden prearranged signal simply stopped the noise and walked away. Neither looked back, and both acted as if they had won some marvelous battle.

Signaling the one teenager who was the most comfortable handling these two, I calmly opened the gate to Gengis' run at the same time the gate to Kubla's run was opened. Simultaneously, we entered those runs and simultaneously we tossed kennel nooses over the heads of two tired but clearly happy dogs. Without saying a word, we simply moved them to new quarters. The next day workers came and repaired the fence.

With the fence repaired we no longer had a paddock with a short fence in the middle, and we moved Gengis and Kubla back. I really expected them to start running the fence line doing their normal fence fighting routine.

They didn't. In fact, they never showed any interest in fence fighting again, and they never showed the least interest in trying to fight at any other time.

I will always wonder just what did happen between the two of them on the day of the not a fight. Surely they both knew the fence was gone. It being missing was the only thing that would account for the volume and the violence I saw. Yet, it was all posturing and neither dog was willing to step across that invisible line thereby taking the fight to the next level. Do you suppose they just used up all the bad words and nasty names they could think of and decided they were now equals?

One other thing came about after that day. The other dogs in the kennel all showed the utmost respect for both Kubla and Gengis. I think they both walked just a little taller, and in time they both went on to finish their Championships, leave the kennel of their birth, and establish lines of their own. Short fences do make for some interesting experiences.

"The Queen had one way of settling all difficulties, great or small. "Off with his head!" she said without even looking around."
Lewis Carroll. (1865)

An Unusual Trio

The three were as unusual a trio to become friends, as a person would ever meet. A 2-year-old Rottweiler, a 1-year-old Labrador and a 1½-year old Golden normally wouldn't find much in common. Granted they were close in age, and two of them were retrievers. Still, a friendship was rather unusual until you took into account just how much each of them enjoyed getting into trouble.

Besides <u>training</u> dogs, one of the things I do is run a day care program for dogs. Better known these days as "doggie day care", it is a program that allows dogs to come to my house weekdays for play, exercise and learning. With today's fragmented lifestyles, it just makes sense that even the family dog would go off to day care or camp. These three were good examples of why day care programs have become so popular.

Whim, the Rottweiler, was coming because she needed to learn how to get along with other dogs and not be afraid of being away from her owner. Tudor, the Golden was here several days a week because he didn't have a fenced yard and needed a place were he could run off some of his pent up energy. Then there was Girl. A Labrador and the youngest of the three, Girl came every weekday because her owner was dealing with a 12-hour workday, and there just weren't enough hours in the day. Girl was what I considered to be a work in progress. She was also the suspected ringleader of the group. When she was around, the three of them were much more likely to get into trouble than when she was absent.

Three nice dogs with good reasons to be in daycare; they didn't come into the friendship easily. In the beginning, Tudor and Girl didn't get along because Tudor wanted to play way too rough for Girl's tastes. Whim didn't get along with Tudor because he wouldn't stop getting right up in her face, and she didn't get along with Girl because Girl was always barking in her ear. Whim really needed a large personal space, whereas the other two weren't interested in personal space at all. Whether you were talking about their personal space or the personal space of others, it didn't matter, because it just didn't exist as far as they were concerned. In the beginning one or more of the three was always losing their free time play yard privileges for breaking the "no fighting" law. Looking back, I suspect all that jail time had a good bit to do with why or how they came to be friends. Seems reasonable to me, you know – that "in adversity we know our friends"* stuff.

Take the time the three of them totally trashed my favorite flower garden. None of them could understand why I totally lost it that day. I ended up yelling and screaming and waving things in the air because I was so frustrated with them and myself for not catching them in time to save the flowers.

When I caught them in the act they just figured the best thing to do was to head for the hills, so to speak. As I approached, they all took off and hightailed it around the house and out of my sight.

I really did have some small reason for being upset with their behavior. First of all, when one of them was here without the other two, there were no problems. When two of them were here without the third, there were still no problems. And for months there had been no real problems, other than the minor battles, when the three of them were here at the same time. Somewhere along the way things changed between them, and I totally missed the signs. I probably missed the signs because I was so busy working on my flower garden. For several weeks I had been weeding, planting and pruning, all the while dreaming of beautiful flowers in bloom all summer. Dreams shattered, I sure wasn't happy to discover the disaster zone they had managed to create. It took a while for me to calm down, and then I went to work, put the garden to rights, put up a fence and went back in the house. All was calm and quiet for the rest of the day.

The next day, instead of causing trouble with each other or some of the other dogs, they wasted no time in heading straight for the scene of the previous day's crime. Crime scene tape in the guise of a lightweight fence prevented any of them from gaining access to all that soft, moist soil. Frustrated with not being able to get into the flower garden, they began a game of chase that lasted for over an hour and at one point or another managed to involve just about all the dogs in the yard.

Finally, hot, tired and winded Tudor threw himself down on the ground right next to the fence. It moved. He wiggled around, and it moved some more. Whim and Girl wandered over to watch. Tudor wiggled around some more, and then he rolled over so he could kick the fence with his feet. It moved. He kicked a little harder, and the top of the fence began to wave back and forth in time to his kicking. Girl found the waving fence top interesting, and when it leaned toward her, she simply opened up her mouth and bit down. Once she had a piece of the fencing in her mouth, she began to pull, back up and pull some more. Meanwhile, Whim got tired of watching the other two, and she grabbed a section in her teeth and began to pull. The fence was starting to come free of the posts, and one of the posts was starting to pull free of the ground.

In nothing flat, Whim and Girl had managed to pull a long section of the fencing away from the posts. The loose section began to bang into Tudor causing him to jump up and back away. He stood there for a time, just watching the tug of war going on between Whim and Girl, and then he simply started to walk forward. When he came to the fence, he didn't stop but just kept on walking. The fence bent, bowed and finally fence posts began to break. Whim lost her interest in the tug-of-war game. Letting go of the piece she had in her mouth, she backed up, took a powerful leap and landed square on top of the fence. All the posts in one long section broke, and the fence bowed toward the ground.

Next, the three of them began to grab the fence posts, pull them free and carry them off to other parts of the yard. The fence itself continued to more or less stand, probably from habit as much as anything else. By this time the day was over and the dogs were all starting to go home. I never noticed the damage to the fence or the loss of so many of the fence posts because… well I guess I was just so sure my little fence would do the trick and besides which it was still standing. (Bet right about now you are wondering how I could have known what happened to the fence if I sent dogs home and never noticed the damage. It's actually easy. I'm looking back on that day and besides which Justice and True showed me how it was done.)

The three dogs were not all together again for a couple of days. During that time the fence continued to stand, which is one of the reasons why I still maintain I didn't notice what had been done to it, nor did I notice the missing posts. It was the end of the week before all three were together again. They waited until all the day care dogs had been checked in and I had gone into the house on an errand before approaching the flower garden. This time, instead of stopping when they reached the fence, they just simply walked through it as if it wasn't even there. Once in, they began to dig, roll and chew on the upended plants. It was a wonderful and most satisfying activity, and then I came to the door.

Talk about mad. It took my breath away as I just stood and stared at the havoc the three of them were causing. When my breath came back, it left again in a monumental yell followed by an ear-piercing scream. I flew down the ramp, waving my cane in the air, yelling and screaming in complete frustration. The three left the flower garden at top speed and headed around the back of the house with me in hot pursuit. The trouble with doing something like that is that the dogs are always convinced you are playing a game of tag with them. Bad move since four-wheel drive always trumps two-wheel drive, and they are going to win. This was no exception to the rule, and finally, completely winded, I gave up chasing and returned to survey the damage.

The rest of the morning was spent with me working on repairs and the three of them taking turns peeking around the edge of the house to see if I was still there. I was. Before the day was done, I had also managed to install a new and stronger fence. That one incident turned the three of them from enemies to fast friends. Truly amazing how a single incident can become so important.

It was more than a week before they again tried anything with the flower garden, but sure enough try they did. Another weekend of long soaking rain had once again softened the ground to where the fence posts weren't really all that tight. That morning when I made my usual walk around the yard, practicing having individual dogs come to me when called, or sit when told, the Three Musketeers, as I now thought of them, were never a part of the group following me. Oh, they would come when I called them, but would then vanish just as soon as they were released. With the morning work done, I went back in the house to wash dog dishes and take care of other jobs. This meant my back was turned, and that was just what they had been waiting and hoping would happen.

The back door had barely clicked shut when the three of them were hotfooting it to the flower garden. A new fence had replaced the broken one. It was a much stronger one, the posts were bigger and imbedded deeper in the ground. Sadly, it turned out to be more of a challenge than a deterrent. Never ones to shirk their perceived duty, the three dogs quickly went back to work. Most of the morning was spent digging and pulling at the new fence. By noon there was one section loose enough for them to squeeze through, one at a time.

Foolish me, I actually thought the new fence would stop the three; this belief let me spend the morning working in another part of the yard all together. To keep my suspicions down each of the three always stopped what they were doing and came every single time I called them.

Thinking about it later, I realized I should have at least wondered about all the mud on their paws, bellies and muzzles. But I didn't. Wonder, that is.

Once inside the fence and actually in the flower garden, they started their version of fun all over again. Only this time Girl noticed the big old-fashioned tub sitting off to one side. I had plans of turning it into a goldfish pond. The work hadn't been started as yet, in part because of the amount of time and energy needed just to repair the damage to the garden. Girl wasn't the least bit interested in <u>my</u> grand plans. She was interested in <u>her</u> immediate plans. Two more days of rain had filled the tub with water.

No body of water, never mind how small, should ever be left untouched. Girl firmly believed this to be a world truth. She jumped into the tub without another thought. The splashing and the tiny grunts of pleasure stopped the others from their dig fest. Tudor put aside his digging, took a couple of quick strides, and jumped feet first into the tub with Girl. Now there were two dogs splashing around in the tub. Whim wasn't about to join them. She hated water and was at a total loss to understand why they were so fond of the stuff. Water was nowhere near as satisfying as mud - good clean, gooey mud. With all the splashing in the tub, the water landing on the ground just helped to contribute to the making of a lovely mud bath. Whim helped the process along by digging at a fast and furious pace until the mud hole was quite large and the plants that had been in that space were tossed from one end of the garden to the other. Satisfied with her labor, Whim stepped into her mud bath just as I stepped out onto the porch and saw what they were doing.

Once again, I was reduced to screaming and, arm waving. "Just as soon as I catch you, you are gong to become cat food. You are all going to the cat food factory! Just wait till I get my hands on you!" I charged down the ramp and headed for the garden.

In their rush to get out, none of them could find nor remember where the opening was located. Panic! Crash! Tudor hit the fence with his chest at the same time Whim hit it with her head. Girl meant to jump over it, but misjudged the height and landed on top of it. The combined weight of all three dogs overloaded the fence and it crashed to the ground. All three made their get away. Another frustrating game of chase followed with this one lasting longer because I was even madder this time. Finally I was so out of breath I had to stop. I also didn't have any more fencing and all the fence posts were broken or had been carried away by one or more of the dogs. My only choice was to sit in front of the garden and guard it from the marauders. One by one they all went home at the end of the day and all I could think was, "thank goodness they are gone."

Over the weekend with the help of friends, the garden received a new, stronger, taller fence with much larger and definitely stouter fence posts. When Monday arrived the Three Musketeers were disappointed to find that even working together they couldn't get the fence down, nor could they budge any of the fence posts enough to allow them to squeeze into that ever - so - tempting area.

On several different occasions during the day, I stuck my head out the door just to check on the status of the fence. Each time, seeing their failure caused me to emit a loud "HA". The three had no choice but to return to the chase and tug games. True, the garden continued to beckon; only this time the fence was strong enough to withstand all attempts at breaching. Stout fences make for good dogs.

* John Churton Collins

"When women are depressed they either eat or go shopping. Men invade another country."
Elayne Boosler

Traveling Companions

Wrap:

"Wrap, settle down", the Boss grumbled and mumbled, "I have to get cleaned up before we can leave."

"I knew it! Just knew it!" My tail was straight up with excitement. "We're going somewhere. Good! Good!"

Finally, after what seemed like a forever wait, all the boarders were sent into the house, kenneled and settled for the afternoon. I stayed out of the way, but close enough to keep an eye on all the proceedings. No sense taking chances on being left behind. After the last kennel door closed, the Boss turned and headed for the bedroom. I trailed close behind.

"Yeah! Yip," I could barely keep quiet, and holding still was starting to hurt. The Boss stepped out from behind the bedroom door holding one of the fancy dress-up collars and matching leash in her hand, and I <u>knew</u> I was going. In an effort to hurry things along, I started trying to push my head in the collar without waiting for the Boss to help.

"Easy there, slow down a little." The Boss calmly removed my everyday collar and replaced it with the one in her hand. Then she slipped a specially made shoulder pack over my head and fastened the chest strap, and finally she checked her watch. Now there was no question about what was going to be happening. We were definitely going somewhere.

Me:

This is really about two dogs, two people and two power scooters spending one summer afternoon at a local mall. It is also about training dogs to work as mobility assist dogs, and perhaps it is also about training people how to work with their dog. The Sunday afternoon in question was hot, humid and a good time to work in the comfort of an air-conditioned mall. I had a new shoulder pack I wanted to try out on Wrap, and so, with the boarding dogs in the house and settled for a comfortable afternoon nap, Wrap and I got in my van and headed for Lauren's apartment.

Wrap:

When we got to the big house, I hopped out and walked beside the Boss to the funny doors. Being able to open a door without help is a good feeling, and these doors made it really easy. The Boss called them automatic doors. What I know is that all you have to do is stand in just the right spot and the doors swing open for you.

"Hi, Munchkin! What'ch up to?" I gave Bitsy a nudge with my nose.

Bitsy was happy enough to see me until she realized the Boss was with me. Turning quickly, Bitsy headed under a chair. "Did she come to take me away? Please tell her I don't want to go."

"Take it easy Fuzzy, we are all goin' somewhere." I did my best to make Bitsy feel better about whatever it was that was about to happen. I was pretty sure we were going on some sort of a travel, just didn't know where.

"I don't want to go anywhere with you or the Boss." Bitsy tried to squeeze just a little further back under the chair. "Just go away. Go away and leave me here."

The Boss didn't pay any attention to her, and so I wandered over and poked her. "Take it easy, I'm telling you we are gonna to do something interesting." Trying to make the fuzzy munchkin more sure of herself could be frustrating at times. About then Lauren called Bitsy to come and get on the scooter. Still trying to make herself as small as possible, Bitsy scuttled over to the scooter and quickly backed up onto the platform.

We all headed out of the building and to a small van in the parking lot. Lauren made Bitsy get off the scooter platform, and she gave Bitsy's leash to the Boss.

"Bitsy, sit". Bitsy sat because it was never a good idea to question the Boss. Then the Boss did something that really made Bitsy feel foolish. She handed Bitsy's leash to me and told me to hold it and stay.

With the leash in my mouth it was a little difficult to talk, but I managed to mumble around it. "Looks like you haven't earned their trust yet. Munchkin, you'd better get with the program." The angle of my right ear let her know just how important I was to her success. My importance seemed to make things worse for her since she started to shake again and with a whine begged me to "please put in a good word for me".

Me:
Since this was the first time the four of us had done something like this, even the loading order had to be worked out. Things such as who would get in first and where they would ride had to be decided. We agreed that the best way would be for the dogs to hold sit/stays in the shade provided by the van while Lauren used the scooter lift to load her scooter and I started the van. Starting the van was a must since it had to be at least 120 degrees inside. No way was I going to load the dogs or myself until things were cooler.

By the time the scooter was in the back and the scooter lift retracted, the van was cool enough for the dogs. Bitsy had never been in this van, and to make it easier for all concerned, I had Wrap jump in first. Seeing Wrap already in the back, Bitsy was more willing to follow, quickly finding a safe place in an out-of-the way corner. Both dogs dropped to a down position when they were told, the rear door was shut, Lauren crawled into the driver's seat, I climbed in and slammed my door.

Wrap:
There was some activity that Bitsy couldn't see, and I really wasn't in a mood to explain. She was just going to have to learn to be patient and deal with stuff. Finally the Boss came over to us, and taking Bitsy's leash from me, she said, "Get in the van".

"Get in what?" Bitsy whined and hung back, not moving because she had no idea what she was supposed to do.

"Come on, Munchkin, follow me," I tossed over my shoulder as I jumped through the open door.

Bitsy followed, all the while moaning, "Oh no! Oh no! Now what should I do?"

"Well, the Boss just told us to down, I suggest you do the same thing I am doing and down right where you are." So she did. "Good choice, Squirt! And stop that infernal noise. You are worse than a puppy!" I turned around to watch the goings on in the front seat, choosing that over having to answer any more of Bitsy's whiny questions.

Me:

At the Mall the unloading process went quickly and without a single hitch. I called both dogs out of the van, moved them off to one side, and giving Bitsy a sit command, proceeded to straighten out Wrap's shoulder pack. Meanwhile, Lauren used the lift to get her scooter out. She then climbed on and turning, closed the van door. Next she called Bitsy to come and hop on the scooter platform. With surprising ease for a first trip, we were quickly on our way to the Mall entrance. I was quite certain this shopping-cum-training trip was going to be a breeze. Bitsy seemed comfortable riding on the scooter platform; Lauren was well focused on what she needed to do; Wrap was being attentive to my needs and I just relaxed, figuring to go with the flow.

Wrap:

When we jumped out of the van, Bitsy was finally in a position to see what was going on. Looking around she made it very clear to me that she really wished she couldn't see anything. Not only were we in a strange and noisy parking lot, but there were people and cars everywhere. Bitsy looked back at the van with longing. No luck there, because Lauren was calling her to come and get on the scooter platform. Watching her behavior was just too painful, so as she crept past me, I growled under my breath, "Listen you, stiffen that spine of yours. We're here to work, not whine and snivel. Get a grip."

Moving through the Mall doors, we were hit with a wall of sound, smell and confusing images. The noise, the echoes, the people, the confusion, the smells— all these things just added to Bitsy's worry about some imagined danger or another. What was happening? What might be going to happen? What was happening right NOW? What might happen later? I wasn't bothered by any of that sort of foolishness, and truthfully I had a hard time understanding why she was having such a problem. The sounds. My ears just wanted to swivel in all directions at once. The smells. My nose was feeding me so much information it all but made me dizzy. So many things to look at, to smell, to feel, they all added up to excitement and fun. Needing to make sure I was seen at my very best, I made sure to pull my ears up as tall as possible; then with my tail straight up, I lifted myself up onto my toes, ever so slightly arched my neck and pranced across the Mall floor. This is the way life should be. "See the people move to make room for me. I am great. I am the best. All move from my path. For goodness sake's Bitsy, do stop your sniveling; you are a headache in the making. Besides, your noise is spoiling the mood."

Me:

We stopped at the Mall Service Desk, I signed out a scooter and with that single act set the stage for all the trouble that would follow us on this excursion. Since I would never be able to keep up on foot due to my bad knee, the scooter seemed to be the answer. Not only would it make it possible for me to keep up, but also, if there were any problems with Bitsy, we would simply trade dogs, and I would work Bitsy until she was back on the right track. At the time it seemed like a good plan, and I couldn't see any flaws. Flaws? Oh yes, there were flaws in the plan. Actually there was one major flaw that almost torpedoed the entire trip.

Wrap:

We stopped at a counter and waited while there was some conversation between the humans. After the Boss did the thing humans call identification, we walked around behind the counter, and the Boss got on a big scooter. I shifted into the scooter heel position, and the scooter started to roll. I knew immediately that I was in for trouble. The Boss didn't seem as sure of herself as usual. As we rounded the corner all I could hear was Bitsy's whining and complaining. "I can't do what you are doing. I'll never be able to keep up. What am I going to have to do? Oh, no! Oh no, please tell them to just let me stay here on the platform. I can't walk. I mustn't walk. Someone will step on me. Help me! Help me!"

"Fuzzhead, just shut up! You are enough to cause pain to a rock. If you weren't so busy sniveling, you would've realized the humans have already decided you need to stay on the platform. So give it a break and be quiet." With a jerk, we rolled into the flow of foot traffic and almost at once the problems started to pile up with blinding rapidity. "Lord, help me, she can't drive this thing!"

Me:

It was a good thing Wrap was the equivalent of a canine genius. She needed every bit of her ability for problem solving with me as the driver of that darn scooter.

First let me tell you about the scooters. Actually the best way to go about the telling is to start by describing Lauren's scooter. Lauren had an old scooter of a type no longer made; too bad, because it was a compact and very zippy little thing. It had a nice tight turning radius, no protruding parts, and was happy to back up as well as go forward.

On the other hand, the scooter the Mall had for lending was almost twice the length of Lauren's scooter. It had this huge double basket sticking out in front. It didn't much care for backing up, and sometimes wasn't sure going forward was such a good idea either. And then there was the turning radius, or the no-turn-turning radius. No neat, tight turn for this monster in need of a football field width to make a simple U-turn. You may then add width to this equation. Lauren's neat, tidy little scooter is narrow and there is space on the foot platform for Bitsy to ride. With Bitsy riding, Lauren and her scooter never got any wider. I, on the other hand, was faced with a great, lumbering monster, and my width was almost double because I always had to factor in room for Wrap to travel beside me.

In spite of these technical problems, we started off for the other end of the Mall and the store where the elevator was located. I started thinking about where we were going and not paying enough attention to how I was "going".

Let me ask you a question. Wouldn't you think that an elevator being used by people in wheelchairs, on scooters or even pushing a baby stroller would better serve the public if it were placed in an easily accessible place? I have never been able to understand why the only readily available means of going from one level to the next in most Malls is by stairs or escalator, while the elevators are located in the most awkward out of the way spot in the entire Mall. Then, to test just what you are made of, they make the access tight, add sharp angle turns, and complete the picture with an elevator that is so small there is barely room for one scooter and a dog, never mind two scooters, two dogs and anyone else. I digress. On the way down the Mall concourse I let my attention wander, at which point Wrap had to do a wild leap to the side to avoid being run over by the scooter that was trying to turn left when I wanted it to go right.

Wrap:

We never did manage to catch up with Lauren and Bitsy until they stopped at the moving room door. By that time all I was able to do was look at Bitsy and roll my eyes. "The Boss needs driving lessons. She is having an awful time driving this thing. I wish I was working for your Lauren right about now."

Bitsy couldn't believe her ears. Wrap not wanting to work for the Boss! She never thought she would ever hear something like that. It gave her yet another worry. What if Lauren decided she would rather have Wrap working for her? Wrap was fast and sure of herself. Bitsy knew Wrap could take her job away in the blink of a cat's eye. These thoughts caused her to start shaking again, and once more she tried to make herself small and then smaller still.

Me:

I want you to understand I'm not really complaining. I'm just trying to explain how it came about that I ended up stuck in the hallway coming out of the elevator. Not just a little stuck, but stuck like the cork in a bottle of old wine. Looking back on the entire event I can't for the life of me remember how or why we decided that Wrap and I should go first. Though in retrospect I have a suspicion it was Lauren's doing and not mine. She knew what was on the other side of the elevator door at the next stop and I didn't. Then again, she is certainly a nice person; surely she wouldn't have sent me into such a maze with no directions on purpose. Or would she?

Wrap:

We all stood in front of the moving room door for the longest time. The Boss and Lauren just kept talking and talking. The door would open, someone would get off, we would have to scoot out of the way, and then the door would close and we would move back again. On and on the two of them talked, humans are like that, the talking part. Always they have to talk and talk before they can do even the simplest thing. If they would only do more listening and sniffing they would be able to do without so much talking. At least, Bitsy had stopped her whining and complaining, so maybe the talking was good for something.

Me:

I gamely pulled onto the elevator with Wrap heeling alongside the scooter. Trouble was riding on the elevator and it hadn't bothered to get off when the door opened to admit us. There was no way I could turn the scooter around in the small interior space. Worse yet, the darn thing didn't stop when I took my hand off the "go" lever. I stopped all right. I stopped when I hit the back wall. Wrap gave me such a look of disgust.

Wrap:

We got on the elevator just as soon as the door opened. I turned around so I would be facing in the proper direction to get off. The Boss just started to fidget, twist and turn. The moving room door shut, and we just sat there. Then the door opened, we didn't get off. We didn't get off because we hadn't gone anywhere. Now I know enough about those little moving rooms to know that the human had to push one of the round things on the wall before the little room would move. The Boss wasn't pushing anything. Actually it looked to me like she couldn't reach the button thingies. I would have loved to help her but there was no place for me to go, so I just stood there and hoped for the best.

Me:

Once I managed to get the scooter stopped, I had to struggle and struggle to get turned around in my seat enough to reach the buttons and push. Wrap was on my left side, where she belonged. The control buttons were behind my right shoulder. The scooter filled all the available space from the back to the front with the little bit of room on my left side being completely filled with Wrap. I would have loved to have had Wrap push that button for me, but there was no way for her to reach the control panel short of climbing up into my lap, resting one front paw on the top of my head and reaching for the button with the other paw. Not something I wanted my dog doing. I mean, who wants their 65-pound dog using them as a ladder to get a job done?

I did finally manage to hit the correct button, the door closed and in due time it re-opened on the desired level. Giving Wrap a heel command, I proceeded to back out. My plan called for me to back out, turn the scooter around and then move out of the way, so Lauren and Bitsy would have room to exit when their turn came. At least I did have a plan.

No luck. Actually, I did manage to back out of the elevator with Wrap moving right beside the scooter. I continued to back up to a spot where I thought I could turn around. To this day I still believe if the tiny foyer had been clear of furniture I would have managed without a hitch. Instead, there were two unnecessary pieces of furniture taking up a large chunk of the tiny space.

Wrap:

I think I saw the problem even before the Boss did. There was even less room on the other side of the door than we had in the moving room. I started looking around for some way to help, since I knew that scooter was going to have to be turned around, and I really couldn't see how the turning would happen. The door slid shut behind us and we were in this tiny little space with no place to go. The Boss kept backing up until she ran into the wall. I moved out of the way as best I could. The Boss pulled forward until she ran into the wall. I moved out of the way again. Then the Boss turned the wheel and tried to move again. Now the scooter moved over and pinned me against the wall on my side. She moved a couple more times and finally was so wedged in that neither of us could move at all.

Do you know what she did at that point? She stopped trying to get out of there and just started laughing. I mean, was she crazy or what? Laughing, when I'm pinned against the wall, and the moving room door is going to open any minute. I can hear it coming and I smell Bitsy and Lauren. We need to get out of the way and she just sits there and laughs. "Why me? I thought the Boss could drive better than this."

Me:

By the time the elevator door slid shut I realized there was a major problem with space or more to the point, the lack thereof. I tried to back and turn and I hit the wall behind me. Wrap gave me one of her "looks". Then I turned the front wheel and BANG! I crashed into a desk. I tried turning the wheel the other way and backing up again. BANG! I ran into the wall. At this point, I was wedged in and couldn't see how I was going to move out of the way. Wrap was totally disgusted with me and the elevator door chose this precise moment to open. Before I had a chance to warn her, Lauren backed out of the elevator and bam! The door closed at once. Trouble got off the elevator at the same time Lauren got off.

Wrap:

Lauren and Bitsy rolled off the elevator. Bitsy peeked her head out and saw the Boss, but couldn't see me. "Wrap? Wrap? Where are you?"

"Pinned against the wall. Can't you see what's happening?"

Bitsy could hear my answer, but still couldn't see me. Lauren was laughing and trying to talk at the same time. Nothing was making much sense except Bitsy knew they had to move. I said so, and besides, the moving room door was opening again, and another wheeled thing with a little person in it emerged, to be followed by another adult human.

Me:

Lauren's scooter was small enough and handy enough to be able to turn around in the tiny open space available. Once she was turned around, she could see me. After staring for a stunned second, she started to laugh. Finally she got control of herself and started making suggestions on how I might be able to get out of the jam. Unfortunately, her suggestions coupled with my poor driving skills only succeed in making matters worse. And they continued to go downhill from that point on.

The elevator door opened once more and a young mother pushing a toddler in a stroller got off. Before she could stop it, the door slid shut once more. We now had two dogs, two scooters, one stroller, one toddler and three adults all crammed in a tiny little space that would have normally been considered cramped if just two adults had been standing there. Lauren and I continue to laugh, and the young mother, after a moment of shock, began to join us. We wouldn't be going anywhere fast, that was for sure.

Wrap:

The Boss was throwing her hands up and laughing. Lauren was laughing. In fact, even the strange lady with the little human had started to laugh. They needed to spend less time making mouth sounds and more time listening and sniffing. There was another person in that moving room, and it was coming back. Bitsy had started to dither again, and I confess I was getting close to losing my patience with everyone. Being pinned to the wall by a huge scooter is no fun. Then the moving room door opened again and out came yet another human. Don't they ever pay any attention to where they are going?

Looks like it is going to be up to me to make things happen. I started poking the Boss. She wasn't paying attention. No surprise there. When she gets in one of the laugh moods, it takes some tough measures to get her attention. I poked her really hard several times and finally had to give her a little pinch. I think it was the pinch that did it. Whatever, she looked at me, and I sent her a mind picture. I looked at Lauren, and I sent her the same mind picture. The Boss missed my point. She looked away, and I had to poke her again. She looked back at me so I was able to send the picture again. I looked at Lauren and started to re-send the picture to her. This time both Lauren and the Boss caught on to what I was trying to tell them. Thank goodness!

The Boss leaned back in her seat as best she could and even moved her feet and legs off to the side. Then she told me I could go to Lauren. There was only one way to manage and that was to jump. So as best I could I gathered myself, then using the wall behind me for leverage I pushed off. Not one of my better jumps, but it did take me over the scooter and the Boss' legs. On the other side there was just barely room for me to land, collect and jump again. My second jump carried me very neatly to Lauren's side. Now that was what I call a good jump! Of course, instead of being impressed with my skill, all Bitsy could do was start whining again about how I was going to take Lauren away from her. Cat dirt! She could be annoying sometimes.

Me:

Just as I started to get control of myself and tried to think of a way out of the jam, darn if the elevator door didn't open again. This time only one person was riding, and she stepped out into our little traffic jam without looking first. I could honestly say it was her belly that joined us first, since she was very pregnant and didn't seem to be in the mood for our silliness. Poor Wrap was squeezed up tight against the far wall, my scooter was filling the entire turn area, Lauren's scooter was taking up all the space by the desk, and the bulk of the space left was filled with the mother pushing a stroller. The new addition to the mess turned out to be a store employee, and she was close enough to the call buttons to be able to call the elevator back. When the door opened she stood in the entrance and effectively gained us some juggling room.

With the small gain in space, it became possible to move the stroller just a little bit. I was able to listen to what Wrap seemed to want, and by moving my scooter as best I could, was able to gain Wrap a little breather room. She used that room to launch herself over the scooter and me. Knowing how solid her send away command was, I told her to go to Lauren while she was literally in mid-air. So as soon as she touched the floor she jumped once more, and landed next to Lauren. Pleased me, pleased Lauren, scared the two women and delighted the baby! Can't say what if anything Bitsy felt about the entire business, I couldn't even see her.

With Wrap out of the way I had just a bit more room, and I was able to jockey my scooter over closer to the wall. This left enough room on my right for the stroller to squeeze passed. By this time the young mother had caught our general merriment over the pickle we were in, and she was laughing as well. With the gain of some more space, I used my scooter to push the desk back into a corner and out of our way. I had gained enough to be able to slowly turn that monster of a scooter around, BUT…

I was facing the elevator again. There was nothing for it but to drive back into the elevator. This was what I proceeded to do, while the store employee continued to hold the door open. The gain of a free path was the signal for Lauren to get out of there. She took Wrap with her and vanished around the corner, her laughter drifting back to me. Sigh, and I still had to figure out how to get out of the jam.

Wrap:

I had no more than reached the questionable safety of Lauren's side, when the Boss began to crash into things again. "Munchkin, does your Boss ever drive like that?"

"My Boss? Lauren is my Boss?" Bitsy was so surprised by what I had just said she totally forgot my question. "Do you mean I am going to get to stay with Lauren?" She actually sat up a little straighter and stopped that blasted whining.

"Hey fuzz for brains, I asked you a question. Does she ever drive like that?"

"<u>My</u> Boss never ever drives like that." Good grief, now I was going to have to deal with a whiny munchkin with an attitude.

By now the Boss had managed to maneuver the scooter up next to the wall, and there was just enough room for that little human carry thing to squeeze passed. This helped to relieve some of the crowded conditions in the tiny foyer. Then Lauren carefully moved her scooter over as far as it would go and encouraged me to move as close to her as I could. At which point, if there had been room for me I would have gladly joined Bitsy on the scooter platform. As it was, I was faced with having to deal with dodging scooter wheels and human feet plus worrying about what the Boss was going to do next. Bitsy was getting far more education than I suspect either Lauren or the Boss had planned for.

With us more or less out of the way and the store lady holding the moving room door open, the Boss drove straight back into the little room. At least that cleared the foyer, and much to my dismay Lauren started down the hall and around the corner. I had no choice, but to go with her. Well actually, I could have refused to go, maybe I should have refused to go, then again the Boss did tell me I was to go, and it is almost always better to do what the Boss says. So I did. Go with Lauren, that is.

Me:

When I drove back on to the elevator, my plan was to use the additional space and somehow get turned around so I could drive out like a normal person. In my backing and turning and backing and turning, I managed to get myself really stuck in the elevator and then somehow get unstuck while never getting turned around. Finally, in desperation I elected to try backing off the elevator and through the foyer, around the corner, down the narrow hallway and out into the store. It was a sad display of driving skills or should I say it was an excellent display of my lack of driving skills? I crashed into the desk. I crashed into the wall. Actually I crashed into multiple walls over and over again, and then, when I did finally manage to turn the corner, the already narrow hallway had been rendered even narrower by the addition of multiple boxes of stuff stacked along one wall. More crashing and banging followed as I caromed from one stack of boxes to the next, until I managed to emerge into the main store.

Coming through the entrance, I was greeted by cheering and Wrap rushing to my side before the scooter had even cleared the opening. The cheering came from ten or so people all either with strollers or in wheelchairs and waiting for me to get unstuck so they could try their hand at the obstacle course style maze representing the only way to an elevator.

Wrap:

Bitsy had never seen me so nervous or worried. I kept straining to see. Then when I couldn't see anything and my ears told me the Boss was in trouble, I poked Lauren and danced my nervous dance. Never did I take my eyes off the entrance to that little hallway.

Finally, Bitsy couldn't stand the strain any longer. "Wrap", she asked, "what's wrong? Where's your Boss? What…?"

"Shut up, Munchkin. Can't you smell there's trouble? Don't you hear it? Humans don't stand around like this unless there is some sort of trouble. I need to be with the Boss, not standing out here where I can't see, much less help."

After my outburst, Bitsy got real silent. She finally noticed the gathering crowd and thought it would be best if she stayed quiet and very small. I continued to attempt to gain Lauren's attention.

Poke. (Smell the trouble?)

Nudge. (Hear the problem?)

Poke, poke, no response. (Listen to me. See what I say.)

Nudge. (I'm about to) Poke. (Leave you) Still Lauren did nothing other than absentmindedly pat my head. I was beginning to despair and decided to just leave Lauren and go looking for the Boss when I saw her scooter slowly backing through that opening. That was the last straw. I left Lauren in a flash and headed straight for the Boss. Forget the rules. Forget the laws. I had to make sure she was safe and not hurt. Jumping up and lightly resting my front paws on her shoulders, I quickly licked her face. "Are you alright?" She tasted ok. I licked her neck. "You didn't get hurt, did you?" She didn't taste hurt. I dropped my front paws to the scooter platform and sniffed her arms and hands. They smelled just fine. I put my front paws back on her shoulders and sniffed her hair and ears. They smelled the way they were supposed to smell. "Please don't do that to me again. How am I supposed to help you when you send me away?"

"Yes, yes, of course, I'm all right. I had to send you away. There was no room for you back there." The Boss was laughing as she pushed me back to the floor.

Bitsy:

Bitsy couldn't believe her eyes or ears. Never had she seen Wrap act that way. For the very first time Bitsy began to think maybe, just maybe things would work out after all. At least, she didn't have to worry about her Boss Lauren doing the strange things The Boss had been doing.

Her Boss. Bitsy had never stopped to consider that Lauren just might be her Boss, her very own Boss. What a wonderful idea if she could make it happen.

Me:

Lauren, Bitsy, Wrap and myself proceeded to leave the store with me only hitting one or two items. Well, I guess I should admit the couple of items just happened to be full size displays that were sticking out in the aisle. You know the sort I'm talking about, they call them end cap displays, and I'm sure it is done to make efficient use of floor space. If only they wouldn't leave them sticking out so far in the aisles. Of course, that is just the poor scooter driver talking.

Wrap:

CRASH! BANG! Bitsy looked behind to see what was happening in time to see that I had managed to move barely fast enough to avoid being hit by items falling off a display rack. My eyes were rolling, and I confess I had my ears pinned back flat against my head. This was not cool. This was not a nice way to travel, this business of having to watch out for things on the floor and things in the air, all while trying to keep track of where the Boss was going to try and aim that scooter next. I could tell by the look on Bitsy's face she was finally glad to be traveling with Lauren. GRRRRR!

Bitsy:

Bitsy could not remember a time when she had seen the Boss make so many mistakes and worse yet, make them all in a row. Poor Wrap. She was so glad she was traveling with Boss Lauren. Boss Lauren. Now that did have a nice ring to it.

Bitsy stopped her musings when she realized they were in some sort of a food place, a human food place, and she had lost track of the Boss and Wrap. She tried poking Boss Lauren to let her know the Boss and Wrap were lost. Unfortunately, the pokes didn't work because she and Lauren still weren't able to communicate very well. Sigh, there were so many things to be learned in order to be a genuine working assistance dog. Sometimes just thinking about it made her tired, and she wondered why she had ever thought it would be a good idea to even apply for the job.

Me:

By now it was fairly late in the day, and since I hadn't had any breakfast, much less lunch, we made the Eatery our first stop. Lauren said she wasn't hungry, but she was thirsty, so this stop would take care of both things. She had gone on ahead and found a table for us. She did try to pick one she thought would be safe for me to use, taking into account my woeful lack of driving finesse. It would have been a safe choice IF it had been next to a wall rather than next to another table with two people sitting quietly, eating and minding their own business.

BANG! End of quiet. I still didn't have the hang of how to stop, and consequently I managed to crash into the table Lauren had picked for us. The crash by itself wouldn't have been too bad had the table stayed put. It didn't. Instead, it proceeded to travel just far enough to slam into the table next to it. Gee, that couple was so nice about the mess. Guess they must have thought I was slightly deranged. Wrap was trying to hide under a table. Lauren was laughing so hard she was crying, and all she could say was, "Two new traveling companions in the making, welcome to the cripple zone. Have a nice day."

Wrap:

Lauren and Bitsy went on to the Eatery, leaving me to cope as best I could with the erratic driving that was slowly taking us out of the store and leaving a hodge-podge of dropped or knocked over merchandise in our wake. The Boss found Lauren because Lauren was waving her arms. I found her because of her smell. It's nice, and she wouldn't have needed to do all that arm waving if they would just listen to me.

As we approached the table, I put both my ears straight out so Bitsy would know that things hadn't gotten any better in the driving department. No sooner did I signal Bitsy than the Boss turned, with no warning at all, and promptly crashed into the table Lauren was saving for us. The scooter didn't stop, but continued on until it was partway under the table, had pushed that table into the table next to it and tipped over a chair. There was so much noise, what with all the crashing and banging, that all human conversation stopped, and everyone turned to stare at us. I decided the smartest thing to do was to get out of the way and took the easiest path out. I dove under another table altogether just as the Boss said, "Oops."

"Oops?" That was the best she could do? Not an "excuse me" or an "I'm sorry", just "Oops". And laugh, both of them started laughing again.

I was reduced to almost a whimper state as I said, "Ah, Bitsy, I don't know if I'm going to survive this shopping trip or not. Her driving skills are getting worse rather than better."

Me:

While eating lunch, we decided that our first stop would be the shoe store. Lauren was in need of a new pair of shoes and her size was difficult to find, dictating she never pass up a chance to at least look. So we left the Eatery and headed for the closest shoe store, where Lauren and Bitsy did just fine. Bitsy was showing more and more confidence, and Lauren was being clearer with her commands. In fact, Bitsy even practiced heeling alongside the scooter for a time.

Guess I'll have to admit that I wasn't doing so fine. I managed to run over poor Wrap's foot, stop to tell her how sorry I was only to stop right on that poor abused appendage. Then in my haste to get off her foot and make amends to her, I managed to drive straight into a shoe display and knock the entire display over. After getting out of that mess all by myself, I headed back to the front of the store and stayed put. All the time my troubles were piling up, Lauren was busy pretending she didn't know me. What a fiasco!

Wrap:

Listening to the human conversation, Bitsy realized they were not going home anytime soon. "Wrap, what's a shoe store?"

I stirred and shifted to a slightly different position. "It's a place where they have lots of shoes and...OH NO...," I paused thinking about the last shoe store I had been in with the Boss.

Bitsy, who had started feeling somewhat braver, began to worry again. "Wrap, what's wrong? Why did you stop talking? Why are your ears sticking straight out? Please tell me what's wrong."

"Listen up, Munchkin, you'll be just fine. I'm the one who needs to worry. Shoe stores are crowded with people stuff and are bad when the Boss is walking." With that I pinned my ears back tight and squeezed my eyes shut. "Bitsyfluff, I'm in deep trouble with this jaunt. The Boss can't drive and we are goin' to a shoe store." A little moan slipped passed my now tightly clenched teeth.

Both scooters were turned back on and started to move toward the Eatery exit. Getting through the crowd didn't prove to be too difficult. The Boss claimed that the rest had helped and her fingers weren't so tired of holding the go lever down. When we got close enough to each other, I relayed that information to Bitsy. With the whine completely gone from her voice, Bitsy said, "I sure hope that's all that's wrong and things get better for you. I don't see how you do it, the job would be way too hard for me."

There was no time for more conversation because we were entering the shoe store. Lauren knew right where she wanted to go and headed that way with us trailing in her wake.

Typical of many mall shoe stores this one had narrow aisles that were filled with people, boxes of shoes, benches to sit on and just general clutter. Lauren on her little scooter managed to get around without a problem. Bitsy stuck her head out just enough so she could see what was happening to me as I trotted alongside the Boss' scooter.

Things were not going well. Moving into the first turn, the Boss managed to hit a large display of shoes, and several boxes fell. In spite of the fact I was moving as fast as I could to dodge all the falling boxes and the shoes that were spilling of those boxes, two of the boxes hit me. One box landed on my head, and the other landed square in the middle of my back.

Realizing falling objects were hitting me flustered the Boss. This caused her to try to rectify things by abruptly reversing direction. Of course the change in direction was not accompanied with her looking in the right direction. The result was that more shoes fell on me, but worse was the fact that I was totally unprepared for the directional change. One of the scooter wheels ran over my front paw as I was trying to dodge yet another falling box. "AIEE"

"OOOOOOO"

"AIEE"

I really didn't mean to yell, much less yell so loud, but I was totally off guard, trapped and it was starting to hurt. My yelling caused the Boss to stop the scooter at once and right on my foot.

"AIEE"

"OUCH"

"OUCH"

My sharp cries rang throughout the store and out into the Mall concourse. The Boss quickly moved the scooter off my foot and started saying, "I'm sorry, oh poor Wrap, I'm so sorry. I didn't mean to run over you. I'm so, so sorry, here let me see your foot."

Grudgingly I held up the abused paw for her inspection. While she was gently massaging it, I took a moment to look around the store. Everyone, and I do mean everyone was staring at us. Curses on my loud mouth! How embarrassing to have attracted attention like that! I jerked my paw back, shook myself and rather grouchily let the Boss know I was more than ready to continue working. I'm a proper Doberman, and there was no way I was willing to allow strangers to think I was a wimp.

Still apologizing, the Boss started forward and promptly got the scooter stuck yet again. This time a kind person came up and moved the clutter out of the way. Lauren and Bitsy had vanished, and I wished I could join them, but duty demanded I stick with the job. I am dutiful at all times. I stayed.

It didn't seem to matter to the Boss who just kept on mumbling, "gotta get outta here, gotta get outta here fast." All the while she was using the scooter to push a bench out of the way and give us, or rather her, a clear path to the door. In order for me to stay with the scooter, I was forced to jump up on the bench, run along it for a length and then jump off. Let me tell you, I thought she was totally losing it 'cause she had never put me in a position like that before. Good thing I am quick and light on my feet.

Once we reached the door to the concourse area, she finally stopped her headlong fleeing. Trouble was that once stopped she went right back to telling me how sorry she was. Where, oh where, were Lauren and Bitsy? I just wanted us to leave.

"Wrap, youwhoooo, Wrap", Bitsy's tiny voice brought me back to focusing on what was happening. "Are you okay? I thought I heard you scream, what happened?"

"Nothin', Fuzzy, not a thing. Nothin' at all happened. You must be hearing things. Dobermans don't scream in public."

Me:

Our next stop was the drug store, a place stocked with things that break when they hit the floor. Before we actually entered, Lauren and I talked about it and decided that Wrap and I would stay at the front of the store right by the door, and Lauren with Bitsy riding would do the shopping.

The thing that was bothering me the most was the fact that somehow the roles had been totally reversed. Instead of me helping Lauren with Bitsy, she was helping Wrap with me. How on earth did that happen?

Just sitting there and waiting when I was supposed to be training didn't make me very happy, so I decided that Wrap and I should do some public relations work. Not my favorite kind of work, but better than just sitting. Very quietly I told Wrap to "go say hello" to a man who was just standing there staring at us.

Wrap:

For a while I tried to listen to what the Boss was telling people as I went up to them and let them pet me on the head. No, make that let them bang me on the head. No matter how long I live, I will never understand how there can be pleasure in having someone bang you on the head. Humans are strange.

After a time I went back to trying to listen to what was being said. I tuned in just as a man ask the Boss how long Weimaraners had been used as helping dogs. Before the Boss could finish her answer, a very loud and rude boy wanted to know if I was a Rockwider. Now I know what a Weimaraner is, and I know I don't look anything like one, so maybe the man needed to wear eye clothes like the Boss does when she is reading.

But a Rockwider? What on earth was a Rockwider? I didn't have a clue, and the Boss was starting to get annoyed. Time to step in and change the focus. I withdrew from the petting frenzy and returned to her. Putting my head on her leg, I gazed up at her face. For some reason this always seems to help her calm down and focus. Sure enough, it worked this time as well.

By then Lauren and Bitsy were finished and had pulled up beside us. After a short conversation, they went off to pay for their purchases, and then we all left the drug store only to head for the Dollar Store.

The crowds of people were much thicker, and it was harder to navigate a path. The Boss was having more and more trouble. For one thing she kept dropping the leash because she had to keep changing which hand was pushing the go lever. Every single time she dropped the leash, I would have to pick it up and then hurry to catch up with her. Keeping track of her, the leash, the scooter and all the crowds of people was not an easy task. I just kept thinking it was a good thing Bitsy was small enough to ride.

Lauren finally called a halt to our progress. Seems we had somehow gotten turned around and all this time had been heading in the wrong direction. This meant we were going to have to reverse direction and go back the way we had come.

"Wrap, are you alright?" Bitsy called out to me.

Putting on a brave front, one ear up and one ear out to the side, I tried my best to sound positive as I assured her I was just fine.

Me:

When we left the drug store we somehow got turned around and headed off in the wrong direction. I really wanted to go to the Dollar Store before we went home, and it was not in the direction we were headed. Once we realized our mistake, we needed to turn around.

Turning around was easy for Lauren. She just zipped that little sports scooter of hers into a tight U-turn and off she charged in the new direction.

"Wait! Wait for me." I had to take this huge, wide sweeping U shaped curve. Of course I misjudged the space. What else? This time my poor judgment caused me to drive straight into a store display that was actually sitting outside the storefront. No way to pretend it was someone else. One part of the display fell on me, and the other toppled into the store, neatly taking out a second display with it. Two women in the store, who had been standing with their backs turned to me, just barely missed being hit. They both screamed.

I suspect their screams were covered up by our laughter. By now I was quite giddy due in great part to all my accidents. Between gasping for breath and laughing, Lauren was complaining about my making her stomach hurt. The two women were convinced they had been almost witnesses to a two-scooter crash. I was far too ashamed to tell them any differently.

I was left to make my apologies to the store manager, and we were finally on our way yet again. When we reached the Dollar Store, it was very obvious that there would be no way for me to drive the monster scooter into the store. In some places the aisles were so crowded there was no room for a person walking, much less a scooter of any size.

Wrap:

After the debacle in front of what looked to be a toy store, we managed to make it to the other end of the mall and this Dollar Store they kept on talking about. As always, Lauren and Bitsy arrived a good bit before we managed to wobble up. Wobble is really the best way of describing our mode of travel. Nothing was done in a straight line or at a steady pace. We jerked, stopped, drifted left, then drifted right, coasted to a stop, started up again. All the time the Boss never stopped with a steady monotone of complaints. I tried suggesting she just park it and walk, but never could get her attention well enough to make myself understood. Humans! Sometimes you just gotta wonder if they are worth all the effort.

As we pulled up in front of the Dollar Store, Lauren managed to drop a bag chock full of new "stuff". I don't have a clue as to just what "stuff" happens to be, so don't bother asking. Bitsy hadn't noticed the bag fall and was in the process of asking me what was going on now when the command she seemed to have some sort of silly dread of came.

"Bitsy, fetch" and Lauren pointed to the small bag resting ever so temptingly on the floor. For a moment Bitsy just stared at the bag in horrified fascination, and then she turned to me with that pitiful, pleading look of hers.

"Sigh! Munchkin, you are on your own. Sigh! Get your sorry self in gear and off that perch of yours and get to work."

"Oh no! Oh, no, no, no!" Bitsy started to wail, "I can't work here! Wrap, please! The humans are watching. Pleassssssse… not here."

"Bitsy, I said fetch and we don't have all day," Lauren was sounding impatient.

Slowly Bitsy got off the scooter and carefully moved toward the bag. Never once did she actually look at the bag. Instead she just kept on looking at me and pleading for my help. Finally, having more than enough of her foolishness I growled, "If you don't hurry up the only help you are going to get from me is a solid pinch on your butt." I backed my statement up with just the tiniest of ugly faces to let her know I meant business. Seeing my face, she hung her head and moved to the bag and oh so very carefully picked it up.

"Bitsy, paws." Good grief! I couldn't believe it. Lauren was still coaching Bitsy on what to do after she picked something up.

"Wrap," Bitsy managed to wail around the bag in her mouth, "please tell her all those strangers are watching."

"Fuzzforbrains, do what you're told and make it fast. I can't believe what a whiny puppy you're being." At this point I stood up and glared down at her.

Somehow, this sternness on my part seemed to give Bitsy some much-needed courage. She returned to Lauren. Standing up on her back legs, she carefully placed her front paws on Lauren's leg and raised the bag up to her. She even remembered to continue to hold on to it until Lauren told her "okay".

Taking the bag, Lauren said a rather curt "good girl" and let Bitsy back on the scooter platform.

Bitsy backed onto the scooter as fast as she could and made herself downright tiny. Drifting out from under Lauren's legs a wee little voice asked, "Wrap, why is she mad at me? I did fetch the nasty bag for her."

"If you call what you did a fetch, then I guess that is what you did. Munchkin, you make it look awful. You look like you hate working for your boss." I shook myself to resettle my shoulder pack and continued. "Listen to me, and don't forget this, cause I'm not gonna' keep saying it. Bosses never, ever want a dog that isn't happy doing the work. So my advice to you is start looking happy or plan on losing your job and then your home."

"Wrap, do you really think that might happen to me?"

"Well, you know it happened to Gift. You were there the day she got fired. Is that what you want to happen to you? I've already seen it happen to the two dogs that applied for the job ahead of you. I'm not telling you what to do, but I suggest you think about it."

Meanwhile, the humans had finished with their conversation. Lauren and Bitsy headed into the Dollar Store, and the Boss pulled off to the side and parked. Thank goodness it looked like we would not be attempting the nightmare of clutter, narrow aisles and no turn-around space for a big scooter. Then much to my relief I realized the Boss had turned the monster scooter off and cane in hand, was preparing to walk through the store. This was something I could handle without a hitch. We moved slowly and carefully up and down aisles. Not a single thing was knocked over. My toes never got stepped on, and the shopping was completed in record time.

Me:

Checkout handled, shopping over, we stopped at the Service Desk to return the monster scooter. I was grateful my flawed driving hadn't totally ruined the entire trip. On the way home, Lauren and I talked about the day and came to the conclusion the time was so well spent we would do it again the following week. I needed all the practice I could get on monster scooter control. Bitsy had taken a giant step forward in the self-confidence department. Wrap had shown me she was ready to step into the shoes of my full time assistant. As always Lauren had demonstrated how her wonderful sense of humor could save the day.

Outside, the heat and humidity continued to slowly par-boil us all, and next week we would try another Mall, maybe this time without the demolition derby by yours truly.

"If you love something, set it free; if it comes back it's yours, if it doesn't, it never was.
Richard Bach

Built for Speed

This poor dog was really one of the sorriest things I'd seen in a long time. Dark steel gray in color, with a short, tight fitting and rather sparse coat, a long thin whip of a tail and a tuck-up so extreme it made you wonder if the rear end was actually attached to the front end. And thin, so thin you could count every rib and see each vertebra; she carried her head so low it looked as if her chin was scraping the ground most of the time. And I was supposed to train this creature? She certainly didn't show much promise in the life category let alone the train it category. But I figured I could at least find out what her story was and then maybe I'd come up with something.

I started with asking about her overall physical condition since she most assuredly didn't look well fed. Was I ever wrong! Seems she was eating 8 to 10 cups of very high quality food every single day. No she didn't have worms, she had been checked over and over again. And no, there didn't seem to be anything wrong with her digestive system, every thing was normal in that area as well.

So failing to learn much of interest in the health area other than the fact that this 40 pound dog was packing away upwards of 10 cups of food a day and not holding onto an ounce of it, I was no wiser. I moved on to exercise.

Now I was getting somewhere. It turned out this little gal demanded to be allowed to run. Not my choice of words but that of the owner, he actually said, "she demands that I run her every single day."

"She demands to be run? Just how much does she run?"

"At least ten miles every day."

"Ten MILES? Did I hear you correctly? You did say ten MILES?"

"Oh yes, we've clocked her when we had to chase her in the car. She can do up to thirty-five miles an hour for really short bursts but most of the time she moves along at about five miles an hour and she is quite happy to do that just about all day if she can get away with it."

"So how do you get her back when she gets away from you?"

"Oh we just get in the car and follow her. That's a big part of the problem. I want her to start coming when I call her and I want to find a place where it will be safe for her to do her running. She used to run the farm next door to our property. But now that land has been sold to a developer and well you know how that goes."

So now I had a handle on the problem. Well, more or less had a handle on it. There was more to the story. Like the fact that this owner wasn't the first owner. And the fact the newest next-door neighbor, a neighbor I might add that had just moved to 'the country' from 'the city', had turned them in for dog abuse.

"Dog abuse? What do you mean, dog abuse?"

"Well look at her. She is nothing but skin and bone and they say we don't feed her enough and we are forcing her to run by chasing her in the car."

By now I was busy running my hands over this little speed demon. Let me tell you, she was all muscle under that skin. Any place on her body that didn't need a heavy layer of muscle was pretty much just skin. This gal was built to run and she also obviously came with a large amount of desire and heart.

"I know I can teach her to come every time but you are still going to have to find a safe place for her to run. I have an idea."

"What?"

"While I am teaching her to come I want you to check out the track at the high school. Find out what times it is in use and what times it is empty. I'm not sure it will work but it's at least a shot in the right direction. She needs to run to stay healthy. By the way, where did you get her and what is she?"

"My brother picked her out of a litter of pups at a filling station about two years ago. The owner said her mother was a birddog and the father was a traveling man."

"That figures. So why didn't he keep her?"

"Are you kidding? He lives in a townhouse and you would not believe what she did to the inside of it before she was even a year of age. We both figured she would be better living with me."

"And?"

"And she was. Well that is she was until the farm got sold and the city people started moving in and now I just plain don't know what to do."

"Humm… With her pointer background, has she ever shown any interest in hunting?"

"No, none at all. All she wants to do is run until she is ready to drop, rest, get up and run some more."

"So what is this little runner's name?"

"You just aren't going to believe it. He named her Miss Wings and we call her Wings."

"Fitting. Think it was a prophecy or is this a case of the dog living up to the name?"

At this point I was laughing because I could almost see her wings, what with the way you could so clearly see the layback of her shoulders. Lack of any excess body fat and no coat to speak of sure makes it impossible to hide the basic structure of a dog. Once again I was hit with the thought that this little Wings was going to have to have an outlet for her need to run.

So Miss Wings came to stay with me for three weeks while we worked on her learning to come when called.

The first day was just about the worst type of pure misery for both of us. Wings spent that first 24 hours trying to leave. She tried to leave the yard, she tried to leave the house, she tried to leave the crate she had to sleep in. I was hot on her heels the entire time.

Of course, using the term 'hot on her heels' was probably not the right one because I stayed out of sight the entire time. No way was I going to become the bad guy with this little gal. Much as I hate using my beloved ecollar for any sort of punishment, I had to make the basic rules clear to her and do it as quickly as possible. That being the case, I set up mirrors all over the place so I could stay hidden and still see what she was doing. Every single time she tried to climb the fence it 'bit her' via the ecollar. When she was in the house she learned that just about everything would bite her if she was foolish enough to put teeth or a toenail where they weren't supposed to be.

Her initial response to the crate she was to sleep in was to hurl herself from side to side and scream. No wonder she was evicted from a townhouse so fast. I mean to tell you her screams of rage were enough to wake the dead. She would screech and scream and the ecollar would bite her. She would be quiet for about 5 minutes and then start all over again. It was four in the morning before she finally decided that sleep was the most reasonable option.

Six a.m. and the buzz of the alarm clock got me started on the new day. With only two hours of sleep I was just praying that Miss Wings would remember at least a part of what had happened the previous day. I really didn't want to have to spend any more time than I absolutely had to on the ugly, unpleasant stuff

I was in luck. Miss Wings stepped out of that crate and actually lifted her head and wagged her tail. Wow that sure was a good sign and it gave me a much-needed boost. Over the next hour I checked in all the day care dogs and let out and supervised all the other boarders. At about 7:30 a young Weimaraner arrived. MissL was another runner, but a runner with a difference. MissL had been coming to me for day care since puppyhood and was also enrolled in one of my classes. She knew to come when called and she seemed to take pride in showing off all the different things she had been taught to do.

After a few minutes of careful circling around each other they clicked. Then again, I never had a second's doubt that they would click. MissL took off and started the first of what was to be many laps around the yard with Wings in hot pursuit. For the next hour the two of them raced each other around what was beginning to look like a racetrack.

With almost a full acre fenced with seven-foot chain link I had no need to worry about where they would go and I knew they would eventually slow down. I was content to just watch and wait.

Along about 9 a.m. MissL was beginning to slow. "MissL, Come", tap, tap on the button of the remote that activated her ecollar. MissL did one of her more spectacular mid-air flips and was now headed in my direction at top speed.

Quick like a bunny I managed to get out the sit command complete with a single tap on the button before I was totally bowled over. MissL slid to a stop and missed me with only scant inches to spare. That sit had actually started about six feet from me and there were skid marks on the ground the entire six feet. MissL grinned up at me, her tail thumping the ground. Wings just looked perplexed.

Considering what I knew about her background and what I had lived through during the past 24 hours, I decided I would pretty much ignore Wings for the rest of the day. Instead of working directly with Wings I would simply reinforce the rules of yesterday and spend all my time on the other dogs in need of training.

At first, Wings ignored me. Then when that got a big, fat nothing from me, she started hanging around. Always moving closer yet poised to run she did her best to gain my attention. Not me, no way, instead I continued my slow stroll around the yard. Every so often I would call a dog to me, praise and release it back to play. As usual well before the hour's walk was finished I had all the dogs traveling in a swirl around my feet. Wings stayed to the far outer fringe of this swirl, but she was there. She could have chosen to stay totally away and she didn't. For two more days I treated Wings to the same indifference while giving her plenty of opportunities to see me with the other dogs.

On the fourth morning it was time for a change. When I let Wings out of her crate I not only put the ecollar on her but I also attached a 15-foot web line, also known as a longe line, to her flat buckle collar. Now Wings was wearing two collars and dressed for work. This morning she would have to work for me before she would be allowed to run her hour's worth of laps around the yard.

Wings was back to being a very unhappy camper, chin and tip of tail doing their best to meet somewhere under her belly. Since I find kneeling to be far too difficult to do on a regular basis, I sit in a chair instead when I work a dog on the first exercise. Leaving Wings in a kennel run, I worked my way around the yard leaving a chair here and a chair there until I had light weight plastic chairs scattered all over the place. Then and only then did I go back and take Wings out.

"Wings, come" and I started tapping the button on the remote. With about every third tap I would repeat the command come. At the same time I was slowly backing away from her until I reached the first of my chairs. Sitting in this chair I continued to call and tap. It must have taken her at least three or four minutes of dashing this way and then that way, only to be brought up short by both a series of taps and the length of the longe line before she ever so slowly approached me. I remained sitting and held out my hand, not saying a word. It took her several false starts before she finally made it to me. Once there I simply gave her a quick and very light stroke on her side and then stood and walked away.

It was a full 45 minutes before I had managed to sit in every single chair in the yard. But by the time I got to that last chair, Wings was never taking her eyes off me and better yet the last time I called her she trotted in to me on the first call. I called that good and quit. I quit by simply getting up and walking away. In fact, I went off to work with some of the other dogs and later when Wings happened to wander up to me, without any fuss or fan fair I leaned down and unclipped the longe line. It was almost noon before she decided to take her hour run.

The days sped past with me increasing my demands on an almost daily basis. By the end of her second week with me I could call her to me when she was in the middle of one of her runs. It still took several taps on the remote and several calls but she was coming. It was time to take this show on the road, as they say.

The first stop was a local tennis court. Not very big, but it would do for a first outing. Getting Wings out of my van I checked both collars, made sure the ecollar was turned on and holding only the end of the longe line, I stepped back and tap, tap, tap, Wings Come, called her out of the van and headed for the tennis court. Once inside with the gate firmly latched I turned her loose. She just stood there, frozen. I took one step and she was off. I mean to tell you that gal launched herself with a speed that just about took my breath away. I let her go.

Watching her run the fence line looking for an opening was like watching a patch of mist on the wind. You aren't sure you even saw it and poof it is gone. I gave Wings time enough to make one full turn of the area and then I started calling her. This is when the ecollar is at its best. You can 'reach out and tap' your dog with such economy of motion. No need to chase them. No more need to walk them down. No need to shout, plead, coax or cajole. No need to worry about whether or not you are going to be interesting, just say come and tap.

Well, actually in this case, I had to say come, tap, tap, tap, come, tap, tap, tap, come. Over and over I followed that same cadence while Wings proceeded to dash from one side of the court to another. This is where patience and its twin confidence are so necessary, if the dog is going to learn. Finally she came to me. Not just at me and then around me, but actually to me. I gave her one slow, gentle stroke down her side and then turned and walked away.

Again, she just stood there frozen only to blast off at top speed. Again, I called her. We continued to repeat the release, run, call, praise, release for a full hour. By that time Wings had stopped her wild dashes and was willing to stay close to me. I called it good and we headed home. This same scenario was to be repeated in different locations a couple times a day from that point on. Slowly, Wings earned more and more freedom.

Three days before Wings was to return home I called her owner and suggested he needed to stop by for a lesson. Of course, he couldn't come until evening and by then Wings was tired from a full day of running by my rules and training. She was quite happy to see him and more than willing to come when he called her. Nice, but I wanted much more for the both of them. If Miss Wings was to keep her happy home she was going to have to make a lot more changes.

The next day we met at a nearby playing field. No fences here and lots of reason to just take off and run. Wings waited until I called her and then hopped out of my van. As her feet hit the ground you could see her start to light up. All her muscles bunched and she started to launch herself for a very long distance run.

"Wings, come." Tap, tap, tap went the button. The muscles all relaxed and she turned her head and looked up at me. We headed across the parking lot toward her owner. He just stood there with his mouth hanging open. Miss Wings wasn't running. Miss Wings was walking and walking proud. I think it was then that he also noticed that she had managed to put on some weight. Not much but enough so she no longer looked as if she was being starved.

We started the transfer and he learned how to push buttons, how to call and how to praise. Wings ever so slowly started to forget me and pay attention to him. How did it all end up?

He developed a taste for jogging and Miss Wings became his jogging companion. With her new found self-control she became much calmer and surer of herself. This change in her made it possible for her to put on some weight and that stopped the neighbor's abuse complaints. The changes gave Miss Wings a home for life and gave her owner a healthy new hobby.

Sometimes when I think back all I can remember about Miss Wings was how she looked when I first saw her. She truly was a lean, mean, running machine built for speed.

"Beware lest you lose the substance by grasping at the shadow."
Aesop

James Would Never Do It

Wren was exactly what a well-bred Chow was supposed to be, but for one thing. She was small, nicely balanced, good bone, great head, gorgeous deep, dark red color and did I mention that she was small? Maybe she could have carried off the small part, since she only looked small when you saw her standing next to another Chow. Maybe she could have carried it off, but she didn't <u>want</u> to be in the show ring. The joke was that all she really wanted out of life was to lie on a couch, eat chocolate bon bons, and watch the afternoon soaps.

For a time, I thought she might turn into my next obedience dog. Not so. Wren had her own views of what she was going to do with her life, and they most certainly did not include any of the things I thought she should be doing. As I said before, her idea of a good life was to spend the day reclining on the couch, watching TV and nibbling gourmet dog cookies.

Wren came from a long line of show dogs, all of whom loved going to shows. On a pre-show Friday evening when all the gear was being loaded, the van readied, and the last minute grooming done, every dog but Wren was bouncing up and down or hanging around the door waiting. They were waiting and hoping they were among the chosen ones, the lucky ones that were going to a SHOW! They made it clear to anyone watching that they thought this business of dog showing was a marvelous thing to be doing. Wren? What about Wren? Wren would silently withdraw from the area all together in quest of an out-of-the-way spot, a dark hidey-hole sort of spot, a not there sort of place that might cause the rest of us to forget or at least overlook her, thereby leaving her at home once more.

Realizing just how much she didn't like the world of the pretty dog, I thought she would like the world of the performance dog, and so, I got serious about training her to enter obedience competitions. Being a Chow, she wasn't fond of constant drilling - but hey, neither am I - so our training schedule was an every other day thing. She started learning to heel in the precise manner necessary for the obedience ring. When I called her to heel she learned that meant to come to my left side, position herself about 6 inches from my left leg, and stay right beside me. Next came the sit - first as a sit in that same heel position every single time we halted. Then she learned it as a position to be held when she heard the word <u>stay</u>.

The stand was a difficult exercise for her to master. Wren wasn't overly fond of being handled and she had rather strong opinions about strangers. Her opinion on strangers touching her was that they were rude and she should just leave. So coming around to any other belief took a paradigm shift in her thinking. She was a Chow after all and anyone who knows a Chow knows just how difficult it is to get them to even consider a change in their true belief, much less actually make the change. To her credit, Wren was willing to at least give my ideas on stand, stay and be touched a try.

Learning to come when called just seemed to fall right into place, but I always had the feeling that when she got to me I was missing something. Even now, looking back to that time, I still wonder just what I was missing. She always held her sit/stay and waited patiently for me to call her. She always came straight to me and sat nice and straight and then looked up at me with a "look". Maybe it was her so very serious face or maybe it was the...oh I don't know what it was but there was definitely something missing.

Finally, the last new exercise – the down - was started. When I introduced the down command, she let me know in no uncertain terms that I should have just taught that one first and skipped all the rest! Being even more thickheaded than the dogs I was working with at the time, I still didn't get the message. Nope, I just continued to work and train with the obedience trial ring and green ribbons dancing in my brain.

Deeming her ready for some practice runs I headed off with her to a series of matches. Matches are not official competitions. Matches are where you go to get in the necessary practice needed to evolve from a dog and a human doing stuff as individuals to a smoothly working team. Since all the matches were for obedience only, Wren didn't realize we were back showing again. She was willing to go along with my ideas. They were a bit more work than she had planned, but at least they didn't include hours and hours of standing around or laying around on a grooming table, multiple baths, rude dogs, rude and strangely behaving humans who seemed to feel they had the right to poke, prod and pull at her. Yes, this obedience thing would be okay, just so long as she didn't have to do it very often.

The very first obedience trial we entered turned out to be held on a hot, sunny day. Not Wren's idea of a great choice, but since it was an obedience trial only, and not part of a big dog show the area was small, quiet, calm and everyone minded their own business. Even the judge touched her in only three places, her head, shoulders and back - none of the poking, prodding, opening her mouth to stare at her tongue and her teeth. No, this judge, while a stranger, was polite enough to make the experience all right. Nothing to get excited about, mind you, but all right. Best of all was the last exercise: for three minutes plus the time it took me to get back across the 30-foot distance, Wren got to do the thing she liked best – lie down. In her case, down meant even her head was down and her eyes were closed, a good and proper position to spend most of your life as far as she was concerned. While the score we received wasn't good enough to be in the top four, nevertheless, it was good enough to be comfortably in the middle of the pack, and it did earn us a green ribbon.

"Wren, you did great! In spite of your attitude towards work in any form, you now have your first qualifying score and a leg toward your Companion Dog title." I got a slow tail wag in acknowledgement and not another thing.

"Check it out! Wren managed a qualifying score and earned a leg today", was my way of announcing I was home.

"Way to go Wren. Want a cookie?" was my son's response to just about anything one of the dogs did.

Wren was more than happy to trot off to the kitchen, collect her cookie, and head for a cool spot in a back bedroom to nibble said cookie very slowly and the spend the rest of the day sleeping. Later she briefly joined everyone else for dinner only to head straight for her kennel and a good night's sleep.

Since I wasn't a complete fool, I knew better than to enter more than one trial on a weekend. The next trial wasn't until the following week. Knowing better than to push my luck, I sure didn't bother her with much of anything that even remotely looked like drill work during the following few days. That turned out to be a good choice on my part, because the following weekend the end of the class saw the judge handing us, not just a second green qualifying ribbon but also a yellow third-place ribbon and a large box of very fancy dog cookies as well.

Pulling into the driveway, I started hitting the horn to announce we had not only returned, but also returned in style. Wren really did deserve a cookie this time, especially since she had won a whole box of them. Even I had to agree she should have at least a couple of them right away. All this happened on Saturday.

Monday evening rolled around, my brain was cluttered with dreams of more ribbons and, I lost all common sense. "Wren, now that you have two of the three needed qualifying scores you are a two-legged dog and there is no reason for you to just lay around the house all the time."

My remark earned me a very squint-eyed look from Wren.

"Starting this evening, I want you to help out in the training classes. Nothing too difficult, you will only have to demonstrate the first step of whatever exercise I am teaching the beginners. At that level you won't have to work very hard – shoot! - you won't even have to think very much."

That didn't even earn me a look, much less a tail wag. Wouldn't you think I might have noticed her screaming lack of enthusiasm? I mean, even in those days, I was supposed to be a darn good dog trainer. Still, I was being sucked into that wishful thinking mode so dangerous to clear thinking. I really wanted to make a name for myself in the obedience and dog-training world, and I wanted to do it with dogs I had bred - not with just any breed of dog but with a Chow - the breed I grew up with, and remembered from my childhood. The breed everyone said couldn't be trained. So when I looked at Wren, I didn't see what she was telling me, I saw what I dreamed of having, and those are two entirely different things.

Three weeks later, we headed off to our third obedience trial. This one was different in that it was being held in conjunction with an all breed dog show.

Unlike a small obedience only competition, at a dog show there is a cacophony of loud noise being supplied by battalions of people all intent on having things "their way". On the other hand, there is a conspicuous lack of manners; both dogs and humans seem to relish being as rude as possible. Why on earth would any sane person want to subject themselves or their dogs to such an atmosphere? The energy, the excitement, and the thrill of winning are the only answers I can give you. But oh, the highs are so very high; you win and feel like you own the world. Of course the lows are as awful as the highs are wonderful. Best not to dwell on the lows.

Anyway, Wren was entered in the obedience trial, her litter brother Warlock was entered in the breed competition, as was her aunt and another distantly related female. Instead of having me all to herself, Wren had to share my attention with 3 other dogs. She was so mad she was actually stiff! When it was her turn to go in the ring, there was nothing I could do to get her loosened up. She laid down when she was supposed to sit. She didn't only move on the stand for examination, she actually turned her back on me! She watched me do a heeling pattern and made no attempt to join me. When I called her to come, she slowly got up, and rather than coming to me, she walked right out of the ring! Going back into the ring for the group stay exercises was not something I looked forward to having to do. Sure enough she was lying down when she should have been sitting. She didn't even wait for me to take a full step away from her before down she went. Then she didn't want to get back up between exercises. It was awful! It was painful to be a part of, and it was painful to have to watch.

I came out of that ring mad - mad at myself, mad at her, and just plain mad at everything in general. That's when I ran head on into James.

James Hunter was a fellow about my age who had only been married a couple of years. He and his wife had saved and managed to buy their very first home just a few months before. The house came with a fenced-in backyard, and James was at the dog show because he now wanted to buy the dog of his dreams. His dream dog was a Chow and he didn't want a Chow that didn't look like a Chow should look. The problem was that he couldn't afford a show dog. Even if he could have, none of the people over by the breed rings would talk to him, much less consider selling him a dog. So he had wandered over to the obedience ring area, spotted Wren in the ring, and was waiting right outside the gate wanting to talk to me as I came out and crashed right into him. Poor guy!

It took me a good half hour before I had cooled off enough to talk to anyone, much less a stranger. In the meantime, James just hung around and talked to Wren. For some reason, she was very happy to listen to him. She even, little by little, moved her sorry self over until she was lying right next to his chair. Humph!

As I cooled off, I couldn't help but listen to James talking to Wren. He was telling her how much he wanted a dog just like her, and that he thought she was wonderful. Goodness, just look at all the things she knew how to do. He didn't know what she was supposed to have been doing in the ring, so what he saw her doing looked just fine to him. Watching them together sure made me step back and take a hard look at what I was doing. That step back was a humbling experience, to say the least, what with Wren making it very clear that she preferred James' company to mine and James so obviously enjoying Wren just for being herself rather than a show dog or an obedience trial dog.

The long and the short of it was that James went home that day with my business card and the instructions to call me on Monday or Tuesday so that we could at least talk. James made that phone call, he came by the house, and then he came by my dog training school. In fact, he took to showing up at the school two to three evenings a week. It got so he was helping out with little jobs, all the while soaking up all sorts of information. He went out and bought himself grooming tools and begged me to teach him how to use them. Now mind you, he still didn't own a dog much less a Chow, yet there he was all but pleading to learn how to groom Chows. So, I started teaching him. Considering how many Chows I had at the time, there were always more than just a few in need of grooming. The extra help was always welcome. Somehow he always seemed to manage to groom Wren.

The weather had first turned cool with the approach of autumn, and finally it was getting down right cold. There were some more shows coming up. Most of them had obedience trials attached to them. I entered several dogs in the breed competition, and sure enough, sufficient time had passed that I had forgotten the reason why Wren still needed one more obedience trial qualifying score in order to earn her American Kennel Club Companion Dog title. Just one more qualifying score and the cool weather was the sort that Chows really love. So I thought surely she could manage, couldn't she?

The morning of the next show/trial was cold, and dark, with the sky full of heavy looking clouds. I hate being cold. The only thing I think I hate more than being cold is being cold and wet. It was cold and then the wind started to pick up. The judging continued. It got even colder and with the drop in temperature came the rain. First a light sprinkle began when there were four dogs to be judged before Wren and I were to go in the ring. Then the sprinkle turned into a steady, cold downpour when there was one more dog in front of us. Then it was our turn. As we stepped out from under the tent and into the ring, the steady rain turned into a deluge by the time we had finished the on-leash heeling pattern. As the judge approached Wren to do the examination part of the stand for examination, gusts of wind began to hammer at us. We got through off leash heeling some how, though I really don't know how, since it was raining too hard for me to see where I was going. I didn't have a clue as to where Wren was by then. Finally came the recall, the coming when called exercise. I left her and sloshed across the ring to take my place on the opposite side. The judge told me to call her. I did. The wind picked up at that moment, and the very heavens seemed to open. It was now raining so hard I couldn't see the 30 feet across the ring. I didn't know if she was still there, much less if she would come!

What seemed like an eternity later, here she came, plodding along, carefully lifting and then placing one foot at a time. As she got closer to me I could see she was traveling by feel alone since she had her eyes squeezed tight shut. Her coat was wet clear through. Water was streaming into her eyes, dripping off the tips of her ears, and running in rivulets off her back. She was one sorry sight. Then again, so was the judge, and I sure wasn't anything to write home about. When the exercise was completed, the judge called a halt to the judging until the rain eased up a bit.

An hour later, still very damp and very cold we went back into the ring to do the group exercises of a one minute long sit and then a three minute long down. Wren had had it with the whole crazy business. She did a one-minute long down and then she did a three-minute long down and of course she didn't earn her third qualifying leg that day.

All the way home I just kept on seeing her doing that recall. It really was impressive. The more I thought about the effort she had put forth and how much she really didn't like the obedience ring any more than she liked the breed ring, the worse I felt. It wasn't as if she was the only dog I had and besides, there was James. He really wanted to give Wren the home she wanted.

So I called James, and he came over. We talked about what Wren wanted, what he wanted, and what I wanted. In the end, Wren got what she wanted. Because I realized that James would never do it. He would never do the things I did with Wren. He wanted the same things Wren wanted. The very next day James came back. This time when he left, Wren went with him to the home she wanted, a home where she actually did get to lay on the sofa all day and watch the soaps.

Because James would never do it. Never require of her the level of effort I wanted. Never make her go to another show or trial she didn't want to attend. What James did do was give Wren a home that in her book was really great. When I hear people saying that once they have a dog they will never give it up, I always remember Wren. How much happier she was when she was in an only dog home where she was treated like royalty. I also kept my promise to Wren and never again showed a dog in really foul weather. I made a promise to Wren that cold, wet day that after seeing the effort she made to do obedience exercises that made not a lick of sense to her. I promised her that I would never again choose to make my dog miserable by insisting on doing something that could just as well wait until more advantageous times.

"There is nothing either good or bad, But thinking makes it so."
Hamlet, II:2

The Crumb Snatcher

Ring! Ring! Ring! "All Good Dogs. May I help you?"

"My dog just bit my husband and the vet said I should call you!" When I hear a statement like that in place of a hello I know I'm in for a long one.

"Sounds like you have a problem. Why don't we start from the beginning? What's your dog's name?"

"Ber. But we call him the Crumb Snatcher most of the time. He's tasted blood now, is he going to kill the baby?"

Hanging on to the phone for dear life, I struggled not to laugh. Well, it was more a case of trying to not laugh and cry at the same time. Where do these strange ideas come from? Instead of doing something to further upset Ber's owner, I asked, "How old is Ber and what breed is he?"

"He's two, and he's a Schipperke." Only she pronounced it She'-pur'-kay, and it took me a beat longer than normal to figure out what she was talking about. Schipperke, pronounced Skip'per'key, are small, all black dogs with sharp foxy faces and no tails. They are busy, nosey, little dogs who usually have something to say about everything, even when they don't know what they are talking about. Ber was a good choice for a name since with their thick, off standing coats and little round butts, Schipperkes do look rather bearish.

Knowing the breed the way I did, I could pretty much figure out how the problems got started. The big question was going to be to figure out if I could change the owner's perception enough to help the dog. I was thinking of how to go about making this change when I realized she was still talking.

"We can't drop anything on the floor and then pick it back up again, unless we wait for Ber to check it out. If it's food, he is going to eat it, and if it isn't food he just may want to chew on it."

"All right. Tell you what; let's schedule your whole family for a consultation. That way we can at least get you started on straightening out the problems."

After making the appointment and hanging up the phone, I continued to sit at my desk trying to figure out how I was going to handle this one. The dog would be the easy part, but what on earth was I going to do with the humans? Of course, the baby wasn't the issue, and I wasn't too sure that the husband was much of an issue, but Lannie Ember was going to be a problem. How best to approach her without my ending up as the villain in a plot not of my making?

What I knew already was that she didn't see Ber as a dog, and only in the past day or so had she even began to see him as anything other than a human child. If it hadn't been for his drawing blood I doubt I would have received a call in time for me to start the steps necessary to prevent the baby from being bitten. I was going to have to come up with a way to introduce the electronic training collar I favored for training without having her react in a totally negative manner. No easy task, since I was pretty sure I was going to be dealing with lots of emotion and not much in the way of analytical judgment. Well, tomorrow would tell the tale.

In the meantime, my next student was pulling into the driveway. I headed out to the training area to meet them. Buck was a big, somewhat goofy, and rather klutzy fellow who was slated to become a full time service dog in the near future. He was scheduled for additional work on his retrieving skills. It wasn't that he didn't like retrieving - quite the opposite, he loved to retrieve. The problem was one of direction, his or ours.

At the ripe old age of fifteen months, Buck had about as much grace and finesse as an out of control freight train racing down a long hill. On the large side for a Labrador, he wasn't in full control of his boundless energy or enthusiasm. He swung back and forth between rushing out to retrieve an object before he knew what he was supposed to retrieve, dashing back and trying to deliver the object to your mouth instead of your hand, or gazing off into space and missing the entire exercise! Without the help of the ecollar, his training would have been slow and discouraging. With the ecollar, we were sailing right along and only once in a while did we hit a bump in the road. Yesterday had been one of those days, with not just one bump but an entire road full of potholes. I had great hopes that a good night's sleep plus the lovely weather would have us back on track today.

While Buck took an obligatory cruise around the yard to check out the message spots, Connie and I worked on our training plan for the day's lesson. Having decided to work on five different articles in five different locations, I had Connie call Buck to heel. One quick tap on the remote button coupled with a heel command and Buck was flying in to Connie.

It was one of those things you see in slow motion; at the same time you are frozen and not able to say a word. I could see it coming and Connie couldn't. Buck was coming in <u>way</u> too fast. Connie needed to give him a sit command to stop him and help him think about what he was going to do when he got to her.

She didn't. By the time Buck reached her, well, it was too late. All I could do was walk over to her and help her back to her feet. In the meantime, Buck rushed around in circles, darting in every so often to take a swipe at any exposed body part with his tongue. He was sorry about the problem, and could he please help?

Back on her feet and no longer wobbling, Connie tapped the button on the remote and called Buck to heel. This time as he charged in, she remembered to tap the button and tell him to sit. She did it while he still had time to slow down and readjust so as to not knock her down a second time. After the rather shaky start, the rest of the training session went zipping right along. With Buck released to cruise the area again, Connie and I spent a few minutes discussing the session and decided that the next day's homework would be to work on slowing down Buck's response to the commands.

Two additional students came and went, and then it was time for all the day care dogs to go home. Another day was over, and I still hadn't figured out how I was going to deal with tomorrow's crumb snatcher. That wasn't entirely true. I knew exactly how I was going to deal with him, I just didn't know how I was going to deal with his owner.

After working with two pretty straightforward and non-demanding students in a row, the time to deal with Ber and his family was on top of me. I studied them as they came up my driveway. I still didn't have a clue on how to approach the issues that were really causing their problems. I mean, how do you tell someone they are going to have to change all their ideas about something and tell them in a way they can accept? This was always my weakest area, and one of the main reasons why I was constantly saying it was so much easier to just take the dogs and work with them.

Crashing my gate was a small circus in furious action. Two adults and a small dog running back and forth while doing his very best to get everyone tied in knots. I had to admire the dog's abilities. Small as he was, his lack of stature wasn't at all a roadblock to his maintaining the upper paw. He was winning and winning handily. I promptly stopped worrying about what I was going to say and hurried to help them make it through the gate in some semblance of order.

"Hi! You must be Lannie and this must be Ber," I reached out and slipped the retractable leash from her hand. Quickly hitting the lock button, I stopped Ber from gaining any more slack line to add to the tangles he was trying to tie into outright knots. Next, I grabbed up as much of the loose line as I could and by dropping the now stationary slack to the ground it became possible to untangle the human legs. With this accomplished, everyone was able to move through the gate and into the yard.

What a mess to have to sort out: retractable leash in a big snarl, husband with a well-bandaged hand, and Lannie herself in a total dither. Missing from this stew was a baby, and I distinctly remembered being told there was a fear of the baby being bitten.

It was a really nice day. I had decided earlier that I wasn't going to spend any more time inside than I had to, so to further my plan, I basically moved my office out to a lovely spot under one of my big trees. It was to this outdoors office I headed with the Embers and their now wildly spinning dog.

By the time we reached the chairs, Ber was not only spinning in circles, he was panting heavily, barking and pretty much out of control in the emotions department. Dealing with this spoiled, pampered pooch had me thinking "thank goodness he isn't any bigger or he'd be a lethal weapon!"

"Poor Ber, look honey, he is about to have another one of his seizures," Lonnie wailed. "Maybe this wasn't such a good idea. He is so upset and..." Lannie trailed off as her eyes settled on Jack and then locked on the bandaged hand.

Well, at least I knew one thing for sure; I was going to have to spend the better part of the next hour acting as the bad guy if any progress was to be made in favor of the dog. More dogs end up in trouble because there is no guidance, or in many cases, the wrong sort of guidance. In all my years as a trainer, I have never yet met a dog that was really comfortable trying to be a human. Of course, I have also never met a human that was really comfortable trying to be a dog, so I guess that sort of evens things out a bit. Poor Ber was being forced to attempt the human baby role, and it was slowly driving him crazy.

"Lannie, I want you to sit on the chair right there. The one that has a leash draped across the seat. No, no! Don't move the leash, you need to sit on it."

See, I pretty much knew from the original phone conversation that I was going to need to have a chair already set up complete with a leash. I had bet the Embers would show up without a leash and was just hoping that if the collar was the wrong size or worse yet, there was no collar, that I would have the right size in my collar collection. Sure enough, all they had was the retractable leash and a very loose fitting harness. By the time Lannie was settled on the chair, I had managed to get the retractable line fully untangled, retracted, and re-locked so as to function as a short leash - not that it mattered much because Ber jumped into Lannie's lap and started growling at me. I ignored him for the time being.

"Jack, I'm going to ask you to play secretary and fill out the paperwork, plus take a note or two." So saying, I handed Jack a clipboard complete with pen, my general information form and a couple of blank sheets of paper.

"Lannie, we are going to have to put a collar on Ber and get him out of that harness before he takes it off and just leaves."

"He doesn't like collars and he doesn't like having the harness on too tight," she whined.

"That's fine as long as he is paying the bills, but until that time you get to decide what he is going to wear and today I get to decide what he is going to get to wear - and it's <u>going</u> to be a collar! Well, actually it will be two collars, but for right now I am willing to settle for just one properly fitting collar."

With that, I whipped out a small flat buckle collar and had it around his neck and fastened before he really knew what was happening. Next, I fastened the leash to the collar and told Lannie to put Ber back on the ground. Instead of following my instructions, Lannie started to stand up so she could free the leash and give Ber more space.

"Lannie, stop right now! Ber hasn't earned the right to have more freedom. I want you to continue to sit on the leash just the way I had it and I want you to put Ber back down on the ground."

After clutching Ber to her breast for a second, she slowly lowered him to the ground. Furious with this turn of events Ber took a quick nip at her hand. From the way she jerked back I had the feeling this was not the first time he had disciplined her.

"Okay, now I want you to unclip the retractable leash and give it to Jack." That turned into a ten-minute struggle, since Ber had now decided that he wasn't going to allow this change either. Things were definitely looking up. If this kept up, Lannie was going to get mad at Ber, and then she wouldn't see me as the bad guy any longer or at least that was part of my plan.

Right about now Ber was in the process of really working himself up to a major blow. He was violently angry about what was going on, and just looking for someone or something to bite. Since there weren't any hands or arms within reach, he turned on the chair and tried to gnaw a chair leg. Nothing. So he tried a second chair leg and in the process managed to get tangled up in the leash. This cut his small amount of freedom by at least fifty percent and started a fit of barking.

What was I doing while this was going on? A big, fat nothing, I just sat on my own chair and watched the battle. As it began to look like the chair would once again prevail, I looked up at Lannie. She was totally frozen in place with a look of panic on her face. Glancing over at Jack, I could see he seemed to be taking the entire scene with more grace. Actually I thought he looked rather pleased with what was going on.

"Lannie, don't you dare touch Ber. He got himself into that mess, and it is his responsibility to get out of it. Besides, as mad as he is right now, if you were to try and help him, he would probably just bite you. Now, while he is dealing with <u>his</u> problems, let's talk a little bit about just what is happening, and what <u>you</u> are doing."

"Doing? Doing? I'm not doing anything and I need to…"

"No! You don't need to help Ber and yes you are doing something very important. You are giving Ber the time and space to learn some self-control and equally as important, some patience. Then you are going to help him learn to pay attention to you and show you some respect."

"I am? He is? I mean, he will?"

"Yes, and you know the best part? You are going to do all those things by just sitting on him every day, twice a day for at least 30 minutes. So tell me about your baby."

"Baby? What baby?"

Now I was confused. I could have sworn Lannie had mentioned a baby during that first phone call. Turns out she had mentioned a baby, but this baby wasn't even a twinkle in anyone's eye just yet. Seeing Jack bitten and bleeding had started her thinking down a chain of 'what ifs' with baby at the top of her list. Knowing there wasn't a baby just yet sure did take the pressure off, and I knew things were going to work out for Ber. I glanced down to see how he was doing.

"Jack, Lannie, take a quick peek. Ber has calmed down, has untangled himself, and is now just lying there quietly. It only took him 15 minutes. Not bad, not bad at all. But be ready, because he is going to start up again right about now." Sure enough, Ber jumped up, tried to climb into Lannie's lap. When that didn't work he started to spin and bark again.

While Ber was busy throwing his second tantrum, I got busy myself and brought out my electronic training collar. Making sure the collar receiver was turned on and the transmitter was set at the lowest possible setting I started explaining just how this training tool worked. Holding the ecollar in one hand I pushed the button on the transmitter with the other hand. The transmitter had thirty-six different levels. Starting with lowest I worked my way up through the levels stopping when I reached 3 since that was enough to make my point to the Embers. I then handed the ecollar to Lannie and had her hold it in her hand just as she had seen me do. Again I started working my way up through the levels. Lannie ask me to stop when I reached level 3 and I told her that is probably the level would end up being most comfortable for Ber as a learning level.

"Jack, you have to feel this. All it does is tingle. Feels like that thing the chiropractor puts on my back when I'm having muscle spasms." Lannie handed the ecollar over to her husband to try.

In the meantime, Ber had stopped his spinning and managed to get himself tied up again. However, he sure hadn't stopped his barking. If anything, it was even louder and was now directed towards me. No slouch this dog! He had figured out that I was somehow responsible for his current predicament.

Considering his attitude toward me, I felt it would only be fair for me to be the one to put the second collar on him. I explained how important correct fit was and how we would never attach anything to this collar since we didn't want to cause the contact points to dig into his neck. At the same time we didn't want the ecollar strap to be so loose that the contact points couldn't make contact. Moving fast I had the ecollar around his neck, buckled snugly in place, and I was out of there before he had a chance to twist around and sink his teeth into my hand. So Ber became a two-collar dog and I moved away just in time to feel the breeze of Ber's teeth clicking together scant millimeters from my hands. Not exactly a lovable sort of dog.

Ber continued to sit and glare at me for another minute or two, and then recommenced his shrill barking. I set the remote on the first level and tapped the button. Ber continued to bark without a pause. I moved the control up a notch to level two and tapped the button. There was a slight hesitation in Ber's bark and then he continued at full volume. I moved the control up again and I was now on the level three. Tap, tap, tap on the button. Ber stopped barking and looked around. He didn't see anything that looked different so he started barking again. Tap, tap, tap on the button, and he stopped barking, shook himself and lay down. There was no panting, no pulling, no fighting and best of all no more barking.

Lannie and Jack looked at each other and then back at me. The silence that followed was broken only by my own dog who was under the tree next to ours and screaming very loudly at a squirrel. Jack took a deep breath and said, "Look at that dog." As he pointed toward my now not only screaming, but also spinning, squirrel chaser.

Lannie's eyes followed Jack's pointing finger and after watching for a moment turned to me, "How long has your dog had seizures?"

"Seizures? She isn't having a seizure; she is just doing her squirrel dance. Watch." And with that I called her to us. True stopped her squirrel game and headed straight for us.

Ber stood up, and as he started to bark, I tapped the button on the remote and he at once laid back down and just watched what was going on. True stepped up to get a long stroke down her neck, and then I told her she could go back to her squirrels.

"With just a little bit of training Ber will behave the same way you just saw True behave. The best part is that he will be much happier than he has been up to this point."

A week later, Connie, Jack and a much quieter Ber showed up for their first formal obedience lesson. It turned out the first lesson went even more smoothly than I had hoped. We were quickly able to move from the long down exercise that was the first assignment into starting the motion exercise of the week. For their first week, they would practice teaching Ber to watch them and to come when he was called. Ber would be wearing his new ecollar from the time he got up in the morning until it was time for Jack and Lannie to leave for work. He would then wear it again from the time Lannie got home from work until it was time for bed. On weekends he would wear it all day long.

"By this time next week Ber will have turned into a very polite crumb snatcher who will be quite happy to share his crumbs with you. Who knows? He might even bring a few to you. Do you have any questions about what you will be doing for homework this coming week?"

They had none and left still looking a bit dazed over the speed with which Ber had changed. Next week would tell me just how much time they were really spending on making the necessary changes. Crumb Snatchers could be turned into Rug Rats and with a little extra work any self respecting Rug Rat could become Captain Marvel.

"How poor are they that have not patience."
Othello, II:3

Mud Heaven

Four days of solid almost never ending rain. Here it was the fifth morning and still no sign of the sun. Now on top of all the rain, the temperature was starting to climb, causing the air to feel like a sauna run amok. I was tripping over dogs in every room; each and every single one of them cranky and restless and just looking for trouble. If that wasn't enough, the phone hadn't rung in two full days. You know that feeling you get when a normally busy phone just sits there, silent as a dry rock? Is the phone broken? Did you forget to pay the phone bill? Do you even have a dial tone? Maybe the rain caused the phone wires to melt? Those were the sorts of thoughts that had me picking up the receiver every so often and just listening to a dial tone.

Ring, ring…with the only sound being a memory of rain pounding on the roof, the ringing of the phone startled all of us.

"All Good Dogs. May I help you?"

"MUD, MUD, MUD!" the voice screamed in the phone. "There's mud everywhere - mud on my new carpet, mud in the kitchen, and now…"

"Excuse me."

"Mud", this time it came out as a whimper.

"Excuse me?"

"MUD!'- a screech followed by a pause on the other end of the line.

"This is All Good Dogs. We train dogs, but it sounds to me like you need a carpet cleaning company."

"Yes, I know who I called. This is Connie, Buck's soon to be former owner."

Buck was a fifteen-month-old Labrador in training to become a Service Dog. At least I thought that was the plan. He could be something of a handful, and Connie did have days when she really doubted they would ever become a team. It sounded to me as if this was one of those days.

"Ah, let me guess, the rain is starting to get to you or him or the both of you. Which is it?"

"It's Buck. He isn't even yellow anymore. I don't have the strength left to give him another bath, and he's slimy brown again. I think I hate this dog. Besides which he won't help me when I need him."

"Look, Connie, the sun is starting to come out. I don't have anything scheduled for this afternoon, so why don't you come on over. Let's see what we can do about your problem. It will only be one day earlier than your regular lesson anyway."

"All right. Just give me a couple of hours to do something about this mud, and we'll be there. And thank you." Well at least she sounded a little less hysterical and a little more in control.

Heaving a sigh, I hung up the phone, opened the door, and let everyone outside. Looking up to see blue sky, all I could think was thank goodness the sun was finally winning its battle with the storm clouds. Heading out the door at top speed went my Doberman, followed by a large, hairy, mixed breed, two Labradors, one Cocker Spaniel, a Golden, a couple of Schipperkes, one Portuguese Water Dog, and a West Highland Terrier. (Told you the house was full of dogs.)

Just as the last dog slipped through the doorway, the phone rang again, and I turned back to answer it. Interesting how the phone seems to need the light of the sun in order to work.

Only an hour later, I happened to glance out the window. What I saw was a dog owner's worst nightmare and a dog's heaven - mud heaven. Mud - mud everywhere - ten dogs totally covered with mud. In fact, all but one of the dogs were the same color. Mud color. They glistened and gleamed in the sunlight. What had started as a wide but shallow mud puddle at the very edge of my parking lot was now a sea of liquid mud.

It wasn't so much the mud sea or even the dogs that caught and held my interest. It was what the dogs were actually doing. Really quite something to watch, they were pretty much taking turns running at the mud. Depending on the temperament of the individual dog, they either jumped in causing a very big splash, or they stopped short, dropped, and slid into the mud.

While it was true they were a total mess, they were having the time of their lives. Only my dog, True, was close to clean, and even she had mud splatters up her legs and on her face. I smiled until I remembered that Connie and Buck were soon to be arriving for a lesson. The memory of Connie's angry phone voice wiped the smile right off my face. Connie's unhappiness about Buck's mud games had little chance of changing when she saw the condition of the dogs in my yard.

I had no intention of even trying to stop all the dogs from playing themselves out in that mud. After all, there was always the hose and as hot as the day was turning I really didn't figure the dogs were going to last much longer. Once they were tired it would be pretty easy to hose the mud off and then let them air dry. Thinking about what I would say to Connie when she arrived left me with the uneasy feeling I had a real problem brewing. Trying to come up with a solution it dawned on me that since Buck still needed work on coming when called maybe the mud wasn't such a bad thing after all.

Yes, working on a combination of recalls and retrieves should be just the ticket. The sea of mud would be a major distraction. Then I got curious as to how many of the dogs out there could be called away from the mud. That thought led me to wonder just how many different combinations of coming when called could I dream up. Boredom flew out the window as I grabbed up my basket full of remotes and headed out the door to try out some recall combinations.

All the dogs were wearing remote training collars. Each ecollar responded to a remote that was marked with the ecollar wearer's name. I was using a basket to carry all the remotes from place to place because I still hadn't been able to come up with a better method. Once I got to what would be my home base while working, the basket was put down and the remotes all lined up with the names showing. I would only actually work one or, at the most two dogs, at a time. It really wasn't a difficult way to do things, once you got the hang of it. Of course I never stop looking for a better way or an easier way, and the older I get, the more I am convinced the better way is the easiest way.

As always, anytime I show up in the yard I am surrounded by a swirl of dogs. Good thing I wasn't planning on going anywhere other than the shower once I finished this session. Between dogs jumping on me, rubbing on me and shaking on me, it didn't take long for me to be almost as muddy as they were. The greeting was over in the blink of an eye and they were all right back at the mud game. I walked over to a nearby table, plopped my basket down, and started arranging the remotes.

Before I ever had a chance to call my first dog, Connie's van pulled into the driveway. You would not believe the expression on her face when she saw what was going on! My wave accompanied with the swiping at my face to get some splattered mud out of my eye didn't improve her expression.

I never did get to try out the various ideas I had on the group, but what I did find out was that every single one of them was willing to come and kennel up when I called them. Oh, there were a couple who needed a tap or two on the remote to help pull them from the middle of the mud sea, but all in all, I was pretty pleased with the results.

"Look at you, you have as much mud on you as one of the dogs! I thought you were going to help me teach Buck to stay out of the mud." Connie's voice positively dripped with sarcasm.

"Well, it wouldn't hurt for you to unbend enough to play in the mud once in a while, but no, that wasn't what I had in mind. Besides, I don't plan on giving any of them a bath, much less all of them. I'll just have them do a stand/stay while I hose them off and then let them air dry while I take a shower to get rid of whatever mud is left on me."

"Just what were you planning for me, or rather for Buck? Did you just figure you would get me over here, and then let Buck play in the mud anyway?" she complained in a decidedly whiny voice.

Goodness, she sure was in a cranky mood. I shook my head as I headed for the gate, only to realize it was still locked. This entailed a trip back inside to get the gate key. It only took a quick glance in the mirror for me to realize I was a muddy mess. So what? It just felt good to be back outside again. After all it would wash off.

"Connie, you know I distinctly remember someone once telling me that mud was really good for your skin. Just think how nice your skin will be after you finish here today." Connie's face puckered up to where she looked like an old prune.

"Come on now, lighten up. I was only teasing. We really are going to work Buck around that mud and not in it." Unlocking and opening the gate, I stepped back so Connie and Buck could come in. With the weather so humid for the past week and the barometric pressure doing an up and down dance on an almost daily basis, Connie's joints were swollen, painful and tended to freeze in a position and then refuse to move. This forced Connie back into her wheelchair. Wheelchair travel was a thing that never made her a very happy camper, so to speak.

Buck, on the other hand, could have cared less. There didn't seem to be much of anything that ruffled him or bothered him or even caused him to change his mind. He was always happy, with today being no exception. There he stood, tail going a mile a minute, tongue lolling out of a mouth that curved up in a big grin, and eyes that lit up when they spotted that sea of mud. This was going to be a challenge on two fronts. His desire to go play in the mud and my desire to let him had to be balanced against Connie's need to have him learn not to dash off to every single mud puddle that might present itself. I suspected we were in for a long, arduous session. And so we started working.

First I worked Buck near, but not too near, that puddle. Poor guy, every single time he had to pass it up he gave it a longing glance. Each glance earned him a tap, tap, tap on the remote button, just enough reminders to keep him moving on the straight and narrow. After each successful pass, I would praise him and then take him back to Connie so she could praise him as well. Finally, we had worked to the point were we were right next to that puddle. The pull of the mud was so strong even I could feel it. He was just managing to say 'no I won't' each time. It was definitely the place to quit.

"Look Connie, this guy has really worked hard. He's earned a break. What's more he's earned a mud break! I'll hose him off when I hose off the rest of them, and then he can air dry right along with them. How 'bout it?"

"Well…"

"I can hear you thinking. You are afraid he will like it too much and want to do it all the time. Am I right?"

"Yes. I wasn't able to get him to come to me a single time yesterday when he was outside playing in the mud."

"Can't say I blame him. I mean, just think about it. Actually, I'll go you one better, let me show you."

Finally I got a slow and very reluctant nod of agreement. She couldn't even bring herself to say it out loud. Well the nod was better than nothing, and I certainly didn't wait nor ask for anything more. I just reached down and gave Buck a slap on the side, told him okay, and walked away. He just sat there, staring first at me, and then at Connie and then at that wonderful sea of mud. A sea I might add, that had been steadily shrinking the entire time we had been working.

While Buck sat there trying to decide just what to do, I strolled over, opened the kennel gates and turned everyone else out.

The mad rush of dogs heading straight for that mud was all it took. Buck was up and in the middle of it before I could even get the last gate fully opened. The interesting part was that, after a couple of passes, each dog left the puddle behind and headed off to other parts of the yard to do other things. I figured it was a good time to start with the clean-up and started calling dogs to me so I could hose the mud off them. Well, I didn't have much hope of actually getting it all off, but figured that I'd get the worst of it and nature in the form of clean, wet grass would do the rest.

While I was calling, hosing, releasing and then calling the next dog, Buck and the other two Labs did their very best to turn themselves into mud pigs. Hum…Mud Pig Dog. Wonder if that might become a specialized breed some day?

It had never occurred to Connie to listen to Buck and reward his hard work with things he asked for or things he showed an interest in doing. Consider how difficult it is for most humans to listen and actually hear what another human is saying. I guess I shouldn't be so surprised about the consistent inability of most of my students being able to "hear" their dog. Connie was neither better nor worse in the listen and hear department. Then there is the look and see department. How many people look at something and don't actually see it? If an owner can look but not see and listen but not hear is it any wonder why their poor dog has so many problems?

By the time I had finished with the last of the non-Labs, I was dripping wet and feeling the need for a break.

"Listen. Connie, I'm gong to scoot in the house and grab a few towels. We are both going to need them. Actually, I need some right now." I wiped the muddy water out of my eyes and headed for the house.

Once inside, the idea of a tall, cold bottle of Coke was just too much; so after grabbing a handful of towels, I headed for the kitchen. When I jerked open the refrigerator door and pulled two bottles of Coke out, I happened to glance down and see that I was dripping muddy water all over the kitchen floor. Joy! Now I would get to mop the floor before this day was over. Oh well, with a little luck maybe I would only have to mop it once. Glasses. Glasses with ice and a twist of lemon. Now that would be a nice touch. Nah, skip the fancy stuff and just get back outside.

Much to my delight, I found Connie had relaxed and now had a smile on her face. She was also covered with muddy footprints. In fact, the most impressive footprint resided smack in the middle of her forehead. The reason for the muddy footprint and the smile? Buck was leaving the mud and coming to her every single time she called him.

One of the Schips or more properly Schipperke, had come back to join the Labs in the mud. He was totally hysterical to watch in action. Tucking that little round butt he would literally fly through the mud. Slipping, sliding, twisting and turning, he was managing to leave the larger, more clumsy Labs in a heap. What's more, he was doing it time after time.

All the Labs would get up, sort themselves out, shake and start to look for him. Then, like some sort of demented fly, here he would come. and never from the direction they expected. Airborne and with his butt tucked in really tight, he looked rather like a cannonball. When he hit the mud, the effect was the same as a cannonball. The Labs would all dive for him, get tangled up and end in a pile. Out would squirt the Schipperke fly, and off he would go, only to lap around and morph back into the cannonball Schip once again.

Handing Connie the cold bottle, I pulled up a chair and joined her to just watch. "Well, are you feeling a little better? When you first called me this morning, I didn't even recognize your voice. Tad bit upset, weren't you?"

"I was so busy trying to stay clean and so frustrated at having to stay in! Yesterday the damp really got to me. I couldn't get out of bed without help, and Buck was being a real jerk." She took a swig of her Coke.

"Do you know what he actually did to me?"

"No. You still haven't told me what happened."

"I tried to get up and was so stiff I couldn't sit up in bed at all. So I tried to roll over, thinking I'd just sort of, well you know, slide my legs off the bed and then get up that way. Couldn't do it."

"So what happened?"

"I called Buck to come help me. He was a total creep." Just thinking about it was causing her to start to cry.

"Whoa, wait a minute. I still don't know what happened. Until I know what happened there is no way we can start to fix it. Just take a deep breath, have a couple sips of your Coke and then tell me." She sipped and sniffled.

It turned out that when Connie called Buck to help her, he had his own ideas about how to help. He had been trained to help Connie get out of bed in several different ways. He could jump up on the bed beside her, turn his back and sit. She could then pull herself up by holding onto his harness. But this was first thing in the morning, and he didn't have his harness on just yet. So jumping on the bed and sitting wasn't going to get the job done.

Another way was for him to jump up on the bed and use his nose to push her legs off the bed. This strategy wasn't going to work either because she was under the covers, and he really couldn't get to her legs.

The third way he had been taught was to stand beside the bed so Connie could put an arm over his shoulders and then pull herself either into a sitting position or off the bed and onto the floor. Once she was on the floor, Buck could help her to stand and then she could sit back down on the side of the bed.

While it was true that Buck had been taught all three ways of helping Connie in a situation like this, and it was true that Connie had been taught how to tell Buck what she needed, that communication sure hadn't happened.

Connie told Buck jump up on the bed. As I told her later, that was her first mistake. Once he was on the bed Connie couldn't figure out how to position Buck so she could pull up since he didn't have his harness on. Buck, being young and just starting out, quickly got frustrated and plopped down, refusing to move anymore. So Connie lay there for a while and fumed. That was her second mistake.

She then tried to get him to push her legs off the bed. This probably wouldn't have been a bad idea except for the covers. What happened next must have been really funny. Buck kept trying to push her legs but with him standing on the covers her legs were pretty effectively pinned in place. She was starting to lose it, he was starting to get frantic, and there was no one around to tell them to stop and take a deep breath. Not stopping and rethinking the problem was her third mistake.

By the time she reached this stage in her story, I knew what was coming, and so had the time to get some control over my own reactions and not burst out laughing.

"He put his nose in the small of my back and shoved me off the bed. I couldn't even stop it because the sheet had gotten tangled around my one arm and my legs were stuck."

"Do you understand?" she wailed. "He actually pushed me out of bed, and I fell on the floor. The sheet and part of the blanket came with me and I was all tangled up. Then he grabbed the sheet and started pulling! He ripped the sheet! When I tried to get him to stop, he just wagged his tail really fast, licked my face and pulled harder."

We watched Buck go head first into the mud and still miss catching the Schipperke.

"I'm not sure I can deal with a dog. Maybe he should go to someone else."

Oh how I wish I had a dollar for every single time I have heard that comment. It always seems to come right before everything clicks into place so that I no longer have to deal with a human and a dog. Instead, I am privileged to deal with that wonderful thing known as a team.

"Connie, just knock it off. Buck not only did everything you told him to do, he went above and beyond what you asked of him in his effort to help you. Think about it." With that I started to smile. Couldn't help it, the picture of Connie on the floor, wrapped in a sheet and Buck pulling on that sheet was just too much. My smile got away from me and turned into a grin. The grin finally started cracking around the edges and I started to laugh. Connie just stared at me. Her mouth hung open for a few seconds and then she, too, began to laugh.

"I guess it must have looked pretty funny." Thank goodness, she was grudgingly starting to get her sense of humor back.

"It probably would have been a winner on the World's Funniest Videos, for sure. What do you think you should have done?" I took a long swig of my Coke and waited.

We watched the dogs for a while longer and finally she said, "I guess I really should have had him come and stand next to the bed."

"Yep, I guess you really should have. Think you'll remember next time?" With that I took the last sip of my Coke and got up to start the business of cleaning up the remaining four muddy dogs. With no rain in the forecast, the last of the mud would be dry by evening and tomorrow we would all move on to other things. Besides, I still had a kitchen floor to mop.

"The only way to have a friend is to be one."
Ralph Waldo Emerson

An Unlikely Pair

Over the years I have seen some unlikely pairs of dogs, and this pair was right up there at the top of my list of unusual friends.

Last came to me as a ten-week-old pup. My job was to get her housebroken, walking on a leash and coming when called. The contract called for her to return to her owners and then come back to me for further training when she was about six months. Last was a Great Dane, ten weeks old, and already as big as a 25-pound Cocker Spaniel that came here 5 days a week for day care.

The Great Dane is a giant breed of dog. If you have never owned or worked with a giant breed puppy, you don't have the remotest clue about the challenges they present. There is the business of housebreaking. Getting any young pup to leave all solid waste outside is not all that difficult. With most pups it only takes a couple of days to get them set on a schedule of feeding and eliminating that takes care of that problem as long as the human is vigilant and follows the schedule.

No, the problem is not the solid stuff; the problem is with the wet stuff. Do you have any idea just how much pee a 10 week old Dane pup can put out? We are not talking about a little puddle here. Oh no, not a puddle, but a flood the size of Lake Erie. Puppies in that age range tend to get busy playing or chewing or napping and don't even realize they need to pee until it is too late and then, here comes the flood. Sounds like someone left the faucet running in the bathroom, and you start running towards the bathroom to turn off that faucet. On the way down the hall, you hit Lake Erie, and your foot goes out from under you. Next thing you know, you have to swim your way to shore! Meanwhile, the producer of said lake is bouncing around the edge splattering droplets of pee on the walls, your face, and all other accessible surfaces.

To avoid the problem, Last spent all inside time tied to my waist. Even so, I still had quite a few lakes to clean up that first week. By the middle of the second week, things were starting to look a little better, not just in the housebreaking department, but also walking on a leash. That old "tie-to-your-waist trick" takes care of more than one thing.

With the housebreaking and leash walking well in hand, I needed to turn my attention to teaching Last to come when called. This second task was quickly solved with the introduction of an ecollar. Now some might want to say that putting an electronic training collar on a 12-week-old pup is wrong or cruel or will ruin the pup. Not so. The ecollar as it is frequently called is just a tool, nothing more, nothing less. Like any tool it can be used with great success, or it can be misused. Success or failure is solely up to the skill of the trainer. Personally, I love using it because I find it to be the gentlest, and surprisingly, the fastest way of training.

I put my ecollar on Last, checked to make sure it was turned on, and then began to look for the level that would get her attention without causing her any discomfort. Level One. Tap, tap, tap and nothing happened. Last continued chewing on a bone she found before I put the ecollar on her.

Level Two. Tap, tap, tap and still nothing. Not even so much as a flicker of an eyelid. The bone chewing continued, and some licking and sucking of the end of said bone were added.

Level Three. Tap, tap…blink, blink goes both her eyelids, the bone chewing stops. I wait. The bone chewing starts again. Tap, tap…blink, the bone chewing stops again. Good. Now I know what level I am going to want to use for this training. With the level now established, I clipped a 15-foot longe line to Last's puppy collar and opened the door.

Outside was far more interesting that any old, dry bone. Last hopped up and headed for the open door. "Last, come" was coupled with tap, tap, tap on the button and a gentle pull on the longe line. Last turned her head and looked in my direction.

"Good girl", I patted my leg and encouraged her to come to me where I stroked her neck for just a second as I reached over and pushed the door closed. After those few strokes I turned away as if to do something else. Last flopped down and started chewing on her bone again. I opened the door and gave her a chance to start outside only to call her again with the tap, tap, tap on the button and the soft "Last, Come".

By the time we had done this a few times, Last was looking at me when the door opened rather than attempting to run just because she could. So the training to come when called was started, bolting through an open door stopped before it had a chance to become habit, and we moved to working both outside and inside. Last was called away from lots of distractions, she was called when there were few distractions, she was challenged with barriers in need of surmounting, and had her confidence built up when the pathways were clear. The challenges and successes built her expectation of success to the point where she always came running to me when she heard her name and the word come.

All was well for the first four days. Then, I swear to you, overnight Last grew 4 inches. When morning came, front legs were no longer speaking to back legs, and the tail had taken over deciding the overall direction of travel. So I would say, "Last, Come", Last would look in my direction, the head would start in my direction as the body parts war got underway. The left legs wanted to go right, and the right legs wanted to travel forward, the tail wanted to take the lead, and the head still wanted to see what was going on.

Last would go down in a tangle of long, awkward legs only to have to spend a minute or so just getting untangled and back into a standing position. By that time the come command was long forgotten. A brisk, happy recall was not going to happen, not today or tomorrow or next week or probably next month. When several minutes have to be devoted to sorting out legs, directions, body parts and then trying to remember just what was going on, the idea of coming when called became an exercise in patience and understanding for the both of us. Is it any wonder why some never do really learn how to come?

Thanks to the ecollar, Last continued to move through this awkward period in her life with as much ease as was possible. By the time she was approaching her first birthday, her major problem was not one of poor behavior but of having to constantly be reintroduced to her body parts. On a fairly regular basis she would set out across the yard running as fast as she could. (After all, any self-respecting young dog knows how important it is to keep up with the pack.) Half way across the yard, and the left front foot would decide to greet the right back foot and shake. The falls were both spectacular and painful to watch. Not a single time did Last ever hurt herself, and she always managed to get her legs untangled and hurry off to join the others. She also continued to respond to my calling "Last, come" in a cheerful manner.

The reports I was getting from Last's owners let me know that all the training was holding quite nicely even in the busy, rather chaotic place they called home. Last was mannerly about open doors and gates and never, ever failed to come when called. She was unfailingly polite when being walked on a leash. Everyone was well satisfied with the results. Maybe too well satisfied, because at 18 months of age change was in the wind.

"We want to get Last a friend and don't want to get another Great Dane", Winnie Spring was saying on the phone. I was listening and at the same time trying to imagine just what dog I should recommend as a companion for Last. I need not have worried on that score because they had already made their choice. A Pug.

"A Pug?" The surprise very apparent in my voice. Then again, maybe my surprise was made obvious by the fact that I repeated myself, "A Pug? Are you saying you are getting a Pug or that you already have a Pug?"

"We already have him and his name is Chance."

"Cha…?"

Laughing, Winnie cut in before I had a change to finish the first word or was it name? "Now before you say anything, the kids named him."

"Chance, huh?"

"Yes. They thought it would be fun to have "Last Chance" and so do I. Wait till you meet him, which is why I'm calling. When can I schedule him for some training?"

A date was picked, and one week later Chance strolled, no make that waddled, into my office and life. He was a hoot, already 16 weeks old, and he looked like an old man, a little no-necked old man. I mean, have you ever really looked at a Pug? Really looked? There is this little round head with two widely spaced, big, slightly bulging round eyes. A mouth so wide it almost cuts the circle of the head in half, a tongue so broad and curled you have to wonder if there is room for all of it in that mouth, and then no neck. The round ball of a head just sits, plop right on the shoulders with no neck. You know intellectually there has to be a neck there somewhere, because the head turns and swivels as if there is a neck, and yet there is no neck - or so your eyes tell you.

Chance just waddled up to me as if to say, "Well here I am, now whatcha gonna do 'bout it?" Oh my, now not only would I be dealing with a Mr. No Neck, but one with attitude!

Attitude was what Chance was all about. He knew he could do anything, and darn if he wasn't right most of the time. It took me the better part of two days to figure out how to put an ecollar on him so he would look comfortable. Right from the beginning, he made it very plain that under no circumstances was I to ever treat him like he was small. From the first morning, he would get in line to have an ecollar put on just like the big dogs. Just because he was short didn't make him small, at least that was what I heard him saying. So ecollar him I did, and I have to say his training was some of the easiest I have ever done. It was that attitude again. If a big dog could do it, he was completely positive he could do it as well. No, make that better.

The one thing that made the training difficult was the humor. Chance had a sense of humor to go with the attitude. Put a bow tie on him, stick a smoked down and well-chewed stogie in his mouth, and you would have no problem seeing him as a stand-up comedian. There were days when I had my doubts about getting the job of training done because, after all, how's a person supposed to train when they are laughing so hard? He did get trained and went home, and it was several months before I saw him again.

When Last and Chance came back to board while their family was traveling, I couldn't believe my eyes. For one thing you could walk both dogs in the space of one. Why? Because Chance traveled under Last, totally and completely under Last, not beside, not following but under.

Yes, you read that correctly. Chance went everywhere with Last and did so by staying under her. Somehow, they had perfected the art of moving together as a single eight-legged dog. I spent a whole lot of time that visit and the following visits trying to figure out just how they did it. You would see the entire pack of maybe 10 or 12 big dogs racing around the yard. In the middle would be a Great Dane and under her would be a Pug. He always ran with the big dogs, was always in the middle of the pack, and never, but never got stepped on. If Last backed up, so did Chance. If Last sat, so did Chance. When Last lay down, Chance hopped up on her back and stretched out.

When anyone asks me about unlikely friends, I just close my eyes and watch an eight-legged Great Dane running across my backyard one warm summer day.

"Thus every dog at last will have his day—
He who this morning smiled, at night may sorrow;
The grub to-day's a butter fly to-morrow."
Peter Pindar: Odes of Condolence

The Grandest Butterfly of All

I can't stand it one second longer. I have to brag just a tiny bit. Some years ago I trained a Papillion named Delta as a mobility assist dog. Everyone made fun of me, telling me I was wasting my time. They made fun of the dog, laughing at him and treating his work as if he was some sort of circus dog. He liked the work and really wanted to learn, although you could tell the teasing was starting to have a negative effect on him.

I really didn't have any place for him in my home, so I temporarily placed him in a foster home. There were two children in the home who cared about him, but other than the children and myself, no one else was interested in taking him seriously. I was really starting to worry about what was going to happen to him. It was obvious to me that even though he liked where he was living he wasn't really happy. He couldn't seem to keep weight on, and he always looked so bedraggled and sad. The children spent time with him trying to cheer him up, and they took to calling him Delta Man. For some reason, he always perked up when you called him Delta Man and then had him do something special.

Some time after I had finished with his training a wonderful 'little person' came through my door. A Pseudoachrondoplastic Dwarf with acute arthritis and only 43" tall. Just the person I knew would show up one day. No, I didn't know her, nor did I know she was the right person. I just had been so sure that the right person would show up and that somehow this little person and Delta would find a way to work together.

Actually, she said she was coming to volunteer to do anything I might need doing. She was going through some hard times in her life and missed having a dog. Just wanted to be around dogs for a time each week as a pick-me-up because she felt that the dogs would help her fight depression.

Me? I looked down at her and thought, "Lady, have I ever got the right pick-me-up for you."

Now there was a goal in sight. Delta's training became serious and moved into high gear once more. Keys, spoons, forks, pens, pencils, paperclips, dimes, paper money, shoes, and telephones were added to the list of things he learned to retrieve. He learned how to grab hold of the end of a sleeve and pull, thus making it easier to take the garment off. He learned that when he was sent for shoes there were always two of them to bring back. This meant two trips for him, and he didn't have to be reminded about the second shoe. We were coming down the home stretch. The training was just humming along, but for a couple of persistent and serious problems.

No matter what we did, Delta still looked unhappy and bedraggled all the time. Papillion is French for butterfly. This little butterfly dog always looked like he had broken, torn wings. Then to top it off, Lauren maintained she didn't like him. She just kept saying he was one sorry looking little excuse for a dog. He would hang his head as he approached her, and she would make some comment about him being sorry looking. This would cause his tail to droop, and that in turn would cause her to turn away from him in disgust.

Since she said she was willing to do anything needed in the way of help, I decided that Delta needed a foster home for a weekend - a long, four-day weekend, at that. The weekend turned out to be a moderate success, so I planned on him having to go back and stay for two weeks. That was even more of a success.

When he came back, it was time for some final fine-tuning; and then the next time I asked her to foster him, I told her it would be for a much longer time. She figured I was talking about a month, and I, of course, was talking about a lifetime. The month came and the month went.

In a flash three more months slipped by, and I started talking about finding a permanent placement for him. Of course, I also knew he had his permanent placement and by this time so did Lauren. She was glad I had tricked her into taking him, because, as it turned out, the two of them had much in common. Having spent their entire lives trying to fit into a world of giants, be taken seriously and allowed to do a worthwhile job, they completely understood each other. Delta became the first toy breed and first Papillion to work as a full-fledged mobility assist dog.

Oh, the tales the two of them could tell! There was the restaurant owner who tried to have them arrested only to find *himself* facing arrest. There was a most educational trip to Atlantic City. It started out as a gambling trip, and it ended up as a gambling trip. But in between, there was a certain Casino that learned about the rights of the disabled to choose their adaptive device, even if that devise just happened to be a 9 pound white, black and tan dog named Delta. They went on boat trips. They survived a car crash together. Lauren protected Delta. Delta protected Lauren. As the years drifted by, the edges began to blur and the two of them moved through life in the seamless harmony of a single being.

This little guy did it all in his ten working years. He earned his Companion Dog title. He worked as a demonstration dog for the Howard County, Maryland DisAbility Awareness Program. Best of all he was an extension of Lauren during that time. Together they fought for public awareness of assistance dogs. Together they worked to break down all sorts of barriers.

In 1999, we were featured in a full segment on ABC's 20-20. It was both fun and hard work to do the taping. It took long days over a period of months before the taping was complete. Delta was already sick, and yet he stubbornly continued to work. Doing everything that was asked of him and then going on to reach for a level of achievement almost beyond understanding.

A suitable replacement was finally located and her training started. Not a Papillion this time, but a little Sheltie girl named Bitsy. Meanwhile, Delta continued to battle the cancer, and at the same time, he undertook to help with Bitsy's training. Once Bitsy was ready to take over, Delta lay down his head and closed his eyes. His time was over, and another was ready to take up the work.

Sadly, the grand scheme of things calls for dogs to have much shorter lives than humans. Delta lost his battle and succumbed to the ravages of nasal cancer. One week later, his owner, Lauren Wilson and I stood side-by-side to accept the American Kennel Club Award for Canine Excellence in his behest.

This award is a most special thing, at least to me. Years ago, I promised his Lauren that the two of them would get the recognition they so much deserved. When I made that promise, I never dreamed it would end with Delta becoming the first dog to be awarded the American Kennel Club Award for Canine Excellence as a Service Dog.

A special posthumous award for the grandest butterfly of them all…The Delta Man.

Don't walk in front of me, I may not follow;
Don't walk behind me, I may not lead;
Walk beside me, and just be my friend.
Albert Camus

To Be His Guide

Tall, good-looking, and wearing a friendly smile, the young man coming through the door was on my schedule for a behavioral consultation. According to my notes he and his wife were having some major behavioral problems with this large, virtually out-of-control young Doberman traveling more or less at his side. Ember's barking almost precluded much in the way of conversation. It was hard to get a true idea of her size, other than large, since her bouncing and lunging had her spending more time on her two hind legs than with all four legs on the floor.

"Hello", extending my hand in an offer to shake his hand, I moved toward Todd. Before Todd had a chance to extend his hand in return, my hand was intercepted by Ember's mouth. Not to bite, mind you, just to hold. Todd turned red and started trying to pull back on the nylon lead attached to her collar. Ember continued to lunge forward, and I calmly removed my hand from her mouth.

"Hi! Maybe you should just come on in and we'll get started. We can worry about social niceties later. So began my time with Todd and Ember...

Todd was what I think of as a "wish it would happen" referral. Referred to me by a neighbor in hopes I would/could wave a magic wand and make

145

Ember over into a model dog. She was a tall, gangly, 10-month-old black Doberman bitch of less than impeccable breeding. Her vigorous energy was driven by a broad streak of willfulness - the very sort of young Doberman who frequently ends up in rescue or the animal shelter when an inexperienced and unprepared new owner finally feels defeated. Definitely not the type of dog you would pick for a first time dog owner, someone lacking in assertiveness, or someone who was sick. Only one word fit Ember and her behavior: Wild. She had the ability to test anyone's endurance, and she definitely had Todd's patience stretched to the thinnest of limits.

I have a number of standard questions I always ask at the beginning of a consultation. They are designed to help me get a feel for what the problems are, and they allow enough time for me to watch and make the beginning of an assessment of the dog, the owner and how they interact with each other. Todd answered all my questions politely and apparently truthfully, but there was an undercurrent that at first I just could not put my finger on.

My questions were answered and yet many times the answer didn't quite fit the question. It was one of those things that seem like torn shreds of mist on a foggy night. You can almost see. Things appear to look normal, yet you just feel something isn't quite right. It was the combination of "not quite right" feeling plus the fact that neither Todd or Ember seemed to be able to sit still for more than a couple of minutes that had me really wondering what was actually going on. I sensed there was a broad swath of information I was not supposed to be interested in and felt as if there was a multitude of questions I wasn't supposed to ask.

In going over the information sheet he had filled out, I noticed he had put 'Sales" as his occupation. "So, Todd, I see you are in sales. What do you sell?"

The pleasant expression on his face didn't change but his voice seemed rather flat, and without so much as the blink of an eye, he responded, "Since Cindy - she's my wife - made this appointment, I've run into several people who bring their dogs to you. Do you really think there is any hope for Ember?"

At the mention of her name, Ember jumped up from where she had been lying by his side and started to paw at his leg. Todd responded by first petting her and then trying to push her away. "Okay, so he does not want to talk about his job", I think to myself while to him I say, "Todd, remember you are not supposed to pet your dog right now, and the only reason for touching her would be to push her away. In this case, I think you will be better off if you don't even try to do that, since it just seems to encourage her behavior." He stopped pushing and just glared at me. Well, at least that was an improvement over the pleasant non-response.

"I see you put down that she is very destructive and noisy. How often is that happening?"

I received a blank look as the only response, so I tried being a little more specific. "Is it a problem on a daily, weekly or monthly basis?"

Todd mumbled something, and I had to ask him to repeat himself. Getting the answer to a single question was a struggle and only after some lengthy digging was I able to establish that Ember's serious behavioral problem cropped up one week out of four.

What was so different about that one 5-day period each month? Well, Todd was gone and his wife wasn't home very much for those five days. The one thing I picked up on was his choice of words. He didn't say he was traveling, he didn't say he was out of town; he just said he was "gone". The other thing about his answer that sort of puzzled me was what he said about his wife. He didn't say she was working, instead he said she wasn't home much when he was gone. Okay, so on the surface it looked as if Ember just plain did not like being left alone so much. I made some recommendations for how to deal with that problem. However, something still was not right.

Did he travel in conjunction with his job? Bang! He changed the subject again. The entire consultation right from the very beginning was choppy and disjointed. Normally I try to keep a casual, conversational tone going since we have an hour and a half to fill. My goal is to see the dog calm, relaxed and settled before the time is up. I make use of an exercise called "Margot's sitting on the dog" routine. The owner is seated in a folding chair with the dog's leash run across the seat. With the dog anchored to the left side of the chair on what amounts to a very short tether, it sooner or later becomes apparent to the dog that lying down beside the owner is a really good idea.

Since the only way the dog has a chance of figuring this out is for the handler to not speak to the dog, not move, refrain from what I refer to as fondling and the biggie – have their mind occupied with other interests, it is a great time to learn about dog, owner, family, problems, even in some cases just casual chit-chat.

So while Todd was working Ember on the "sit on the dog" exercise, I was trying to keep a conversation going and I kept receiving signals indicating more than fifty percent of what I wanted to talk about was somehow off limits. Know what happens when you have a sore tooth? You just can't seem to keep your tongue away from that spot. Well, I just could not stay away from the off-limit topics; but at the same time, I realized I was not supposed to be asking about them. Why? Why was he so loath to say anything at all about his job? I didn't have a clue. What was so different about this young man sitting there in front of me with his shaved head and baseball cap? He sure was no skinhead even if his head was shaved.

As the session wound to a close, it dawned on me that, not only did he not have any hair on his head; he had no eyebrows or eyelashes. I let my gaze slide to his arm, and sure enough he had no hair on his forearm; and now that I was thinking in those terms, I noticed he was lacking even a faint shadow of a beard. The session drew to a close. The next appointment had been scheduled, and Todd was on his way out the door.

"Wait!" I called out. Rushing up to him and casually brushing Ember out of my way, I stood on tiptoe and snatched his hat off. Ha! Now all the questions were answered, and I totally understood the undercurrent I had been feeling.

"Okay, Todd, I still have a little bit of free time. Lets you and me go back in, sit, and really talk for a few minutes. Let Ember loose to run around the training floor. She can't hurt anything, and there isn't much that could get her in trouble."

He glared at me for a minute, grabbed his hat, slapped it on his head, and headed back the way he had just come. Once we were both seated I didn't bother trying to pick my words carefully. Not me, no one will ever be able to accuse me of being a diplomat.

"Now then, let's stop being coy. Just what is your prognosis? Are you going to beat it? Where are you being treated? How long have you been sick? And just what form of cancer do you have?"

"What?"

"You heard me. You've been diagnosed and are being treated. So just what is the prognosis?"

After he got over his shock, he wanted to know how I had figured out what was wrong. "Well," I said, "it was pretty easy once I realized you didn't have any eyebrows or eyelashes."

"What does my problem have to do with Ember?"

Again, that was an easy question. "Ember is very sensitive to your every movement, right down to the smallest twitch of the corner of your mouth. I started watching you and realized you were missing more than just the hair on your head. Now that kind of hair loss is normally associated with chemotherapy, and you only get chemotherapy if you have cancer. So you must have cancer. Moreover, I am willing to bet that Ember misbehaves when you go to the hospital for your treatments. Am I right?"

The answer was a very reluctant yes. Yes, Ember was all but impossible to live with when he went for treatment.

"Todd, usually chemo is done on an out-patient basis. You go to the treatment location in the morning and you come home in the afternoon. Then you get the dubious pleasure of being really sick for a couple of days before you hopefully start to feel a little better. How come you are gone for an entire week?"

It turned out that Todd was an in/out patient taking part in a clinical trial. His was a rare form of cancer and a cancer that normally only struck young children. At 27, he was now technically too old to remain a part of this research program. However, he was not only the oldest subject in the study, he was also the longest living. Consequently, he was still being treated through the study.

At first, each time he went to the hospital for his treatments, I kept Ember and worked with her. My plan was to turn her into a super companion, one that would stay by Todd's side and give him whatever comfort it is possible for a Doberman to give.

When Todd was home and feeling able, he and Ember would come to my school and spend an hour or so training. As the months slid by, Ember's obedience got better and better. She continued to be very much in tune with Todd and seemed to know exactly how he was feeling. Finally, the time came when Todd could no longer walk without the aid of a cane. He hated having to use a cane. He said it made him look crippled, and if he looked crippled, it meant he was losing his battle.

I had already taught Ember to retrieve in anticipation of what I knew was coming. That retrieve paid off. Every single time Todd would throw the cane down in disgust, Ember would cheerfully pick it up and hand it back to him. He would mumble and grumble about it; but at least he was using the cane, and we didn't have to worry so much about him falling.

Ember was no longer a problem at home when Todd was in the hospital. Why? Do you think it was because of all her training? You are right if that is what you are thinking. However, wrong if you think she was being left at home or even with me the entire time. Todd's wife was allowed to bring Ember to visit. How? Why?

The idea of using therapy dogs in health care settings was just starting to come of age. At the hospital, two dogs were the icebreakers. One of them was Todd's Ember. Ember helped pave the way to the beginning of something that grew into a wonderful program. In the beginning, Ember was snuck onto the Pediatric Oncology unit via back stairs and service elevators.

There were a whole lot of people, employees, volunteers, researchers, and even visitors who knew about the stealth visits. Not a single one of them reported the presence of a dog to the hospital administration. That alone was something of a minor miracle. The staff was fascinated with how having a dog around seemed to make it easier for so many of the children.

Finally someone in administration got wind of what was going on. Can you imagine our surprise when, instead of telling us to stop, they agreed to meet with us to talk about visiting dogs. After many meetings with the authorities, a program was developed to allow a small, carefully picked group of dogs to visit the Pediatric Oncology Unit twice per month. A Doberman was single-pawed responsible for bringing an entire therapy dog program to a prestigious health care institution. From the tiny beginning in the Pediatric Oncology Unit, the program grew and grew.

Sadly, as the therapy program got stronger, Todd got weaker. Finally, nothing more could be done for him, and he could do nothing more for the program. He was released and sent home. He was sent home, but not abandoned. Doctors from the study continued to follow him and make sure he had all the pain relief he needed. And Ember?

Ember continued to stay very close to Todd. She monitored his every move. Indeed, she seemed to understand when Todd needed her help to get up. When he needed his cane, she was there to hand it to him. She knew exactly where the cancer was and carefully sniffed that area many times each day. When Todd was in pain, Ember stretched out beside him, and used her body to apply both pressure and warmth. This helped to ease the pain. It meant he didn't need quite as much of the heavy opiates now necessary for pain control. This in turn meant he was able to do more things and one of those things was enjoying his baby daughter. And always, always there was Ember, quiet and attentive, ever watchful.

In the fall of that last year, the day came when Todd could fight no longer. In spite of the devotion of Ember, the love of a wife and child, and the support of modern medicine, the cancer won. The night Todd died, Ember howled for several hours. She had to be bodily removed from the room before the funeral home attendants could remove Todd's body. After the hearse pulled away and Ember was allowed to return to the bedroom, she hopped up on the bed and would not move. She stayed there for a day, and then during the hustle and bustle associated with a household when someone dies, the front door was left open. Ember saw her chance and shot out the door. Out the door, straight into the street and under the wheels of a truck she flew at top speed, refusing to heed the cries and commands being shouted. She was dead before the truck had stopped rolling.

Wherever they are, I am sure that Todd and Ember are still together, and I am sure she was here just to be an escort for Todd. I do not have a name for the type of assistance Ember provided; I just know it was a very important assistance because I think she was sent to be his guide.

> "A friend is one who walks in when others walk out."
> **Walter Winchell**

Don't You Dare!

"All Good Dogs, good morning."

"Don't you dare steal another cookie! You hear me?"

Hearing that I knew it had to be Lucy Higgins. Lucy was having more trouble than anyone I have ever known when it came to food-stealing dogs. Comfort certainly was a sweet dog, who unfortunately had a very sweet tooth. If it had sugar in it, and it was even remotely within her reach, Comfort would find a way to do a grab and gobble.

Truth to tell, even I was beginning to despair of ever getting the problem solved. All the while poor Comfort was looking more and more like the Goodyear blimp and less and less like a Standard Poodle. It can be so frustrating to all concerned when the dog is more determined and a darn sight more clever than the owner! This was the case here, and I was reduced to being a sounding board and hoping I could somehow help guide the two of them through what I knew was going to be a difficult few months.

I say it that way, because in my mind I was sure that as Lucy began to adjust to her new life as a single person, she would manage to get a grip on Comfort's thieving ways. I really liked Lucy, and I loved her dog's name. That name came about because Al's job had caused him to do a lot of traveling. They had decided to call her Comfort since her job was to keep Lucy company when Al was out of town on business. Visa, who had been

Al's dog, died of old age shortly after Comfort was added to the household and now Al was gone as well. His life cut abruptly short when he became a victim in the crashing of a high-jacked plane. Lucy felt that Comfort was all she had left.

If Comfort wanted something to eat, she got it. If Comfort wanted a share of Lucy's meal, she got it. If Comfort wanted a share of the evening snacks, she got it. The two of them were just blowing up in the weight department.

What do you say in a case like this? "Hello! The food won't bring him back!" Even though true, it would be a cold harsh thing to say. So, instead, I kept encouraging Lucy to walk Comfort, to train, to drop by when they were lonely. Now, I didn't have a clue whether Lucy was calling me because she wanted to do something about the thieving canine or because she just wanted to talk.

While listening to Lucy ramble on about nothing in particular, I let my mind drift back to when I got to see Comfort for the first time. At four months of age, she was best described as a gangly ball of black fluff on stovepipes. She already had that wonderful, elegant Standard Poodle movement. A glide rather than a walk took her from place to place at high speed. Watching her move around my yard, I was almost able to forget why I have Dobermans instead of Standard Poodles. Then my mind focused on all that incredible mass of puppy coat, and I remembered one of the major reasons why I had chosen a drip-dry breed. All that killer grooming ate into good training time.

My mind snapped back to what Lucy was saying.

"…and I told Al I would show her and earn the obedience title you are always talking about."

"I'm sorry Lucy, I missed the first part of what you just said - one of the dogs, you know."

"Oh, I was just saying that maybe I should get you to start coaching me so I can show Comfort. I did promise Al I would show her, and I really don't want to send her away with a handler so I thought that maybe…"

"Of course, what a great idea! Let's set a time right now and get you started in the next couple of days."

"Well, actually I was hoping you could start me now."

I really should have said no. I knew by saying yes I was just being… a what? An enabler? Gag, I hate that term! Besides I knew how Lucy felt, I understood why she was still talking to Al even though he was no longer there to answer her. Plus I was sure she would start to get stronger even sooner once she had a goal. So with that in mind, I told her she could come for a lesson at 7 p.m.

"Can't I come sooner? Please, I really need to get out of the house"

Knew it; I just knew it! Lucy was trying to run again, and I wanted to say, look I'm just a dog trainer, not a therapist. Instead I said, "Listen, if you want to help me send all the day care dogs home, feed all the boarders, and then feed me dinner you can come now. Other wise, I'll see you at 7."

"I'm on my way!" With that the line went dead.

Oh well, at least I would get dinner out of it and someone to help with the yard clean up.

I stared off into space remembering when I first met Lucy and Al. They had only been married a short time and Lucy was trying to come to some sort of an understanding with Al's dog. A little non-descript sort of dog that Al had found beside a dumpster as a very young puppy. Pup ended up being named Visa, because as Al put it, "…for the first three months I had this pup I was constantly having to pull out my Visa card to pay for something else he needed."

Anyway, Visa really didn't like Lucy and went out of his way to make life miserable for her. In what they claimed was a last ditch effort to save their new marriage, they came to me for help. (There's that counselor thing rearing its head again!) My solution was simple and to the point: Lucy and Visa were enrolled in one of my classes. As he pulled out his Visa card to pay for the lessons, Al had joked that it looked to him like he should start calling Lucy Visa2. I had said, "Don't you dare!" And we all laughed. Now thinking about that day just made me sad.

Al, Lucy, my husband and I all seemed to hit it off, and we ended up becoming friends. It got so we would get together a couple of times a month, go out to dinner, and then end up at one home or the other for a game of cards. The fact of the matter was we really didn't pay much attention to the card game. Most of the time none of us had a clue as to what the score was, we just used the game as an excuse to spend an evening laughing and talking and teasing.

Al was quite the actor, always jumping up to act out parts of whatever story he was telling. He would play most of the parts himself and use Visa for the remaining pieces. Visa had a long list of tricks and would execute each of them flawlessly for Al. They were in much demand as party entertainment and Visa's ability to take very subtle cues from Al made what they did look like magic.

Lucy never was able to get him to do a single trick, although in time they did make peace with each other. Visa minded Lucy in all the day-to-day need to know ways. It was just that he seemed to feel the act that he and Al did whenever Al was telling a story was a thing not to be shared. I used to tell Lucy not to worry about it since Al was a good storyteller. Besides Visa wouldn't last forever, I never dreamed I was forecasting the future for both of them.

Just about the time Lucy and Visa were making peace with each other, my husband died very suddenly, and I was faced with dealing with all the hard choices that go with widowhood. During that period, we just seemed to lose touch with each other. Lucy really didn't need to bring Visa to class anymore, and the card games just weren't as much fun with one person missing.

A honking car horn snapped me back to the present. Lucy was here and I headed for the gate to unlock it and let her and Comfort in.

"Get back! Everyone back! Come on in. Comfort, come."

"No jumping. Hi! I thought it would be nice to order a pizza for dinner. Is that okay with you?"

"I guess so. I have a couple of beers in the refrigerator that will taste good with a pizza. Actually, one would taste good right about now, even without a pizza. Help me get everyone inside, kenneled and fed first."

"Let's order the pizza first. That way it will be here by the time we are finished feeding, and we can eat."

"Lucy, I thought you wanted to start working with Comfort. Sounds like you really came here just to eat."

"Not really. Just think, if I call and order the pizza now, and then we feed, and the pizza gets here just as we are finished feeding... Well, we can eat, chat for a while, and then work some. Now that's an efficient use of our time."

"Uh huh, more likely you will be too full, and Comfort will be too sleepy for either of you to work! But hey – it's your dime this time - so okay, we'll go with your plan."

So Lucy phoned in the pizza order (large with extra cheese plus mushrooms and onions), and I got stuck with finishing the yard pick-up duty. Then followed the noisy and somewhat chaotic period called feeding time. Sure enough, just as I placed the last food pan in the last crate, a knock at the front door announced the pizza delivery. Lucy went to pay for the pizza, and I headed for the kitchen and the cold beers.

Pulling the beer out of the refrigerator, I realized that the last time I had done this was just a week before Al was killed. Lucy and Al had stayed after Comfort's class, and we had ordered a pizza. For some reason, remembering that evening made me start thinking about all the fun evenings we had shared when there were four of us. Bother! Girl, don't you dare go there! If I kept going with this line of thinking, I would never get another thing done for the rest of the evening. Slamming the refrigerator door, I headed for the living room determined to think about now and the future rather than the past. In my rush to get out of the kitchen and away from the memories, I totally forgot glasses for the beer, paper plates or napkins.

"Hey, don't worry about it! The beer probably tastes better straight from the bottle. The pizza delivery boy brought plenty of napkins, and we can manage without paper plates."

"Well, you sure are in a different sort of mood. Is this good or bad?"

"I told you. I talked it over with Al, and I really am going to finish Comfort's training and get the titles on her. And we really are going to start this evening, so no more than this one beer, okay?"

"Okay with me. Did I hear you say titles, as in plural rather than singular?"

"Yes, I remember how much you hate the beginner's class, and how much fun you always say the advanced classes are. So I thought I would start right out with the advanced stuff and skip the beginner stuff. After all, you are always saying how smart Comfort is and how fast she learns stuff."

"Uh…Lucy, it doesn't work quite that way. You don't get a choice. You have to start at the beginning with the Novice class and then move in an orderly fashion into the Open class and then on to Utility. Since I choose to believe you are really serious this time, we will start with Novice. And we will start 15 minutes after we finish eating. Okay?"

Novice, Open and Utility are the names of the American Kennel Club obedience trial classes. At each of these levels, it takes three qualifying scores earned under three different judges to earn a title. This means in theory it would be possible to earn a U. D. or Utility Dog title in nine shows. In practice it takes many more tries, since, as my Grandmother used to say, "there's many a slip twixt the cup and the lip." The first or Novice title is properly called a C. D., which stands for Companion Dog. The second title, the one earned in the Open class, is called a C. D. X., which stands for Companion Dog Excellent, and the final title is that of the Utility Dog.

So Lucy was thinking of going all the way. Great. Now if I could just keep her from getting discouraged, she should have a good time, and end up with a really well trained dog. I figured along the way both of them would end up losing some weight. Seemed like a good deal to me.

Imagine my surprise when fifteen minutes after Lucy poked the last bite of pizza in her mouth, she hopped up and announced she was ready to work. So work we did, and for the next hour I walked her through the exercises required in the Companion Dog routine.

"When do I get to work Comfort? I thought this was for both of us? Why do you have me out here running around with a broom in my left hand?"

"Look Lucy, you are going to be the team leader, and as the leader you had better know what you are doing, where you are going, and how you are going to get there. Furthermore, Comfort doesn't need to be nagged half to death while you are blundering around trying to figure out how to exchange one of your two left feet for a right foot! So let's give the forward, about turn one more go. Okay?"

"Well, I guess. I thought it would be more fun than this."

"I told you the Novice class material was boring. What I will promise you is just as soon as you learn and then you with Comfort start working as a team, we will move on to the fun stuff. No waiting around to finish your C.D. before we start training the retrieve. I promise."

157

Lucy still looked doubtful, and I was beginning to think I needed to try a different way of teaching her how to do that about turn. Remembering how hard it could be to figure out where to put your feet and when to turn you shoulders, never mind your head, I decided that having Lucy walk a visible line would be the best way. I got out one of my long lines and laid it out on the ground.

"Lucy, here's what I want you to do: I want you to walk this line. No you don't have to put one foot in front of the other, just walk along the line. When I call for an about turn you still have to stay on the line. Think you can do that?"

"Sure, that's easy."

"Are you ready?"

Silence.

"Are you ready?"

More silence.

"Lucy, when I say 'Are you ready?' you are supposed to check your dog and then answer my question."

"I remember that, but I don't have a dog right now. All I have is this stupid broom."

"Yes, I know that. But we are practicing, and you need to get into the habit of answering the questions the judge will be asking you. So, are you ready?"

"Yes, I'm ready."

"Forward." With that command from me, Lucy started forward stepping off on her right foot.

"Stop!"

"Now what's wrong?"

"Lucy, show me your left foot."

Lucy lifted her right foot from the ground.

"Huh, Lucy show me your other left foot. The one next to the broom."

"Oh. I forgot."

"I noticed. So go back to the start point, and let's try again."

On and on we worked. Forward. Halt. Forward. About turn, halt. Forward, Lucy use your other left foot, halt. By the end of the hour Lucy was exhausted and happy. As she put it she now knew how to walk. Of course I spent the last few minutes of the hour telling her that quite the contrary, she still didn't know how to walk. All she had done was learn how to move forward, about turn and then halt. In her next coaching session we would work on two more turns and maybe the halt.

"What do you mean, learn to halt? Isn't that what we've been doing all this time?" Lucy took a deep breath. "So what am I supposed to do with Comfort while you are making me poke along learning how to walk with a broom? I don't even use a broom at home."

"Ah yes, Comfort. What you will be doing with Comfort is to continue to train her to respond to your commands. That will be what we work on during your regular training lesson. No more of the maybe she will, maybe she won't stuff. We will get serious about the training. Think you are up to all this?" I was tossing out a challenge and I knew it.

Sure enough, Lucy took the bait, and we were on.

Three months later, Comfort looked to have lost at least 15 pounds, and I was pretty sure Lucy had lost at least as much. They were both looking great, and they were both working great. Lucy had figured out a way to remember the difference between her left foot and her other left foot! Comfort was back to that wonderful gliding gait that a good Standard Poodle has.

I was about to suggest starting to train the retrieve when Lucy threw me a real curve. It seemed Comfort was so pleased with the results she was getting when she stayed in heel position that she no longer wanted to be anywhere else. In fact, it was almost impossible for Lucy to leave Comfort long enough to manage to do the recall exercise. Long before Lucy could get the required 30 feet away and turn to call her, Comfort was trotting up to heel position. Both the sit and down stays had pretty much become a distant dream and even the stand was becoming shaky.

What was going on? What's more, how did I miss the subtle warnings to tip me off that a problem was in the making?

Actually, I had a pretty good idea as to the answers for both questions. It was really easy to miss the warnings because it was just so wonderful watching Lucy and Comfort as they worked on heeling. They made it look like a dance, and in just three short months they already looked as if they were joined together. It was beautiful to watch, and it must have been beautiful to do because they both certainly did enjoy it. In fact, that is what was going on. They were enjoying the heel dancing so much they didn't really do anything else except when they were with me.

Lucy had moved Comfort into a position that was totally out of balance. All Comfort really knew how to do was be next to Lucy in heel position. She was even forgetting how to play with the other dogs when they came over. Major problems in the making, and I had just the thing to fix it before it got any worse.

"Lucy, have you been practicing the place training you learned way back in the beginning?"

"No, there just didn't seem to be any reason to practice it. With Al gone, Comfort sleeps with me so I don't need to send her to a different bed. And I just don't have any desire to entertain the way we did when he was alive, so I don't have company anymore. With no company, there really isn't any reason why Comfort should use her basket in the family room when I really like having her on the sofa next to me. When we are out training, we mostly work on the heeling because you said the heeling was going to be 80 of the 200 points, and I don't want to lose any of them."

"Well, keeping the 40 points for the on leash and the 40 points for the off leash heeling is a wonderful goal. The problem is you've forgotten the other 120 points. Remember, you have to earn 50 or more percent of the available points in each exercise, and you have to successfully complete all the exercises in order to earn that leg or qualifying score. Comfort has to learn to hold a position away from you. If you are going to make it into the more advanced classes, you are going to have to teach her to leave your side."

Which was how and why we ended up spending a couple of weeks just working on place training. Then we went on to start teaching a working retrieve, and it was another couple of months before we got back to working on the novice stuff. But that's a story for another time.

"Slow down and enjoy life. It's not only the scenery you miss by going too fast – you also miss the sense of where you are going and why."
Eddie Cantor

Thornton's Done It Again

You really need to let me tell you about Thornton, although they stopped calling him by that name after a while. They ended up calling him Thorn, and somehow it sure fit. He could be a thorn in anyone's side in a heartbeat. The way I first heard about him was from a neighbor, not a neighbor of mine but a neighbor of Clayton and April Stadd.

According to this neighbor, within a week of the time the Stadd's had moved into their townhouse at about 7:30 a.m. almost every morning you could hear the first of the cries.

"That dog is loose."

"Will someone please catch Thornton?"

"Shut that door. Oh no, grab him! He's got the baby's bottle again."

"Thornton, get back here."

"T H O R N T O N!!!!!!"

Doors slamming all around the court - screams, cries, and, if you looked out the window, you could usually see two or three people chasing after a small, white, black and tan whirlwind. This would go on for about thirty minutes, and then Thorn would drop whatever he had stolen and head for home, complete with an owner in hot pursuit and still yelling at him.

Curious about what sort of dog this was and just what was really going on, I started asking more questions. It turned out that Thornton or Thorn was a Jack Russell Terrier; although my student pronounced it terror rather than terrier. From his overall behavior, she suspected he might still be a puppy. He was definitely a young dog and he didn't have a lick of training. We both sort of tut tutted the sorry state of affairs and went on with the lesson.

Several weeks passed before I heard anymore about Thorn. This time when my student came for her lesson, she had a totally different story to tell.

"You should be getting a call from April Stadd today."

"Who?"

"Last night we held a meeting of everyone that lives on our Court and told the Stadd's they had a choice, they could move, get rid of Thorn, or come to you for training. We can't stand it anymore."

"Thanks for the referral, I guess." I never know what to make of referrals of this sort. It means if the person does call me, they aren't going to be happy about having to make the call. If they do elect to come to me for training, they're going to fight me every step of the way. Not the greatest way to start a relationship, and not something that leads to a good learning environment. Most of the time referrals of this sort end up with the person not calling me or calling me and then changing their mind.

I didn't get a call that day; in fact it was more than a week before I heard from April Stadd. By that time I had pretty much forgotten who she was or why she was going to call me. I certainly didn't stay in the dark for long. Seems my student and several neighbors had paid her a visit just a few minutes before April called me. She was in a real panic since this committee had been less than pleasant about what was going to happen if something wasn't done about Thorn. Actually, it was pretty funny, but I guess I wouldn't have been laughing either if I had lived in the neighborhood.

Early summer had arrived. The kids were out of school. Around here early summer means warm with low humidity. That translates to no need for air conditioning. Everyone had their front door standing open, even the few that didn't have storm doors. Doors standing open are always a bad mistake with a dog like Thorn living in the neighborhood. With him around an open door was going to turn into an invitation to major trouble.

"I'm afraid they are either going to kill Thornton or do something awful to us or both."

I didn't even bother to ask just whom the "they" might be. Not since I knew April was one of Thorn's owners. Instead I ask, "So what did he do this time?"

"This morning he managed to get out the front door again. Honest, I have tried to keep him from getting loose. I thought if I could just manage to keep him in and only walk him on a leash they would forget. This morning he chewed through his leash. When I opened the front door he just shot out."

"And?"

"And just about everyone else's dog and all the kids were out in the circle playing. Thornton ran out to them. Before I could catch him, the other dogs were chasing him. But it gets worse." She stopped talking, and all I could hear was heavy breathing.

"Okay, so he got out, you chased after him, the other dogs joined him. Then what happened?"

She caught her breath and continued, "They all started running around the circle. Everyone was chasing and screaming, only two dogs came to their owners, all the rest just kept running after Thornton. He ran into one house with all the rest of the dogs following him. They wrecked the living room and then ran back outside. I almost caught him but he got away again."

"Where did he go next? Did you notice if any of the other dogs had been caught by then?"

"He just ran next door and ran in that house as well. The other dogs? Caught? I don't think anyone was trying to catch any of the other dogs. Besides there must have been at least 10 kids all chasing after the dogs, and the dogs were all barking and the kids were all screaming. It was awful."

"So what happened when he ran into the next house?"

"He ran through the living room and the dining room, jumped up on the table in the kitchen, and stole a piece of toast. Two other dogs actually followed him up on the table. Then they all headed back outside and ran all the way across the circle to a house on the other side and chased the cat that lives there."

"Well, all I can say is that with all this running into the street, it is a good thing you live on a Court. How did you catch him?"

"I didn't. He just got tired or lost interest in what he was doing or maybe he got thirsty. Anyway he up and ran home. So then I had to chase a half a dozen dogs out of my house, plus assorted kids. And now I am going to have to pay for all the damage he did."

"Damage? Just what sort of damage did he do? Besides steal a piece of toast, that is."

With that April started to cry. Oh no, not another crier. Why me? Why do I always seem to end up with the criers? Part of me knows the answer to the question, but even acknowledging the answer doesn't do anything more that raise more questions.

It seems that dear little Thorn, because in my mind he was turning into a thorn, had knocked over and broken a lamp in one house. He then proceeded to knock over, then trample a plant stand full of orchids in another house. The final bit of damage did have to do with the stolen toast. When he and his buddies jumped back to the floor from that table, they managed to send everything flying. This caused most of the dishes on the table to end up scattered across the kitchen floor as pieces of broken pottery. Talk about a thorn!

"April, I really think that the best thing for you to do right now is schedule an appointment for a behavioral consultation. This will at least get you started working on a more positive relationship than you presently have. It should also help to begin to patch up the damage done in you neighborly relationships."

"I just don't know what to do. He was first in his class in the puppy training class. Now he goes to puppy play school a couple days a week. All his report cards say he is the best puppy in his play group."

"Oh, I'll just bet he is. And I'm pretty sure that is a big part of the problem. Too much play and not enough responsibility - so let's get you scheduled for a time. I will need to see all of you, that means we will need to schedule a time that works for both you and your husband." We made a date for the very next day. Her husband was going to take a couple of hours off work just for the appointment.

When April and Clayton Stadd showed up with dear little Thornton the next day I don't know what I was expecting, but it wasn't what walked through my office door. A sort of an Ichabod Crane with Kartina Van Tassel by his side and tucked under one arm like a football was the terror known as Thornton.

Clay, as he was called, was at least 6′ 5″ tall. Soft-spoken, rather shy and he couldn't have been more than 25. April was pretty much the opposite being a good foot or more shorter and while not fat nor even plump I would have to describe her as soft, rather round, very pretty and very young. Which leaves Thornton. Now in truth, that was a piece of work. Thornton was wearing a bright red harness and attached to the harness was one of those awful retractable leashes. Thornton was struggling, squirming, snarling and barking. He was the perfect picture of a spoiled little dog in an evil temper. All I could think was, "…and here comes trouble".

"Let's get you settled and then we can talk. Do you have a collar for him?"

"Oh, he won't allow us to put a collar on him, so we use the harness." I couldn't tell from the tone in April's voice whether she was bragging or apologizing.

"Umm…Well, here he will wear a collar and just learn to deal with it. Clay make sure you are holding him tight, because I am going to put one of my collars on him."

With that I just went ahead and put one of my regular buckle collars on him and then for good measure put my ecollar on as well. Since I got in and got out again fast enough, he didn't get a chance to bite me; but I was left with the strong feeling that, given the opportunity, he sure would have enjoyed a sample a taste of my blood.

"Now that we have him collared, let's get you in a chair. That retractable leash will have to go as well. You may borrow one of my leashes for the time being." At the same time I was talking, I was arranging the leash across the seat of a chair and attaching it to the buckle collar.

"Okay, now who is going to be in charge of this thorn?"

April and Clay looked back and forth at each other and then at me. "Hey, don't expect me to make that decision. It's totally up to you, but one of you is going to have to be the one in charge."

Finally, April took a very tentative seat on the very edge of the chair, and Clay put Thornton on the floor. No sooner did those feet touch the floor than Thornton was in action. He lunged, he pulled, he flipped himself, and then he started screaming, only to follow that with a dive under the chair, back out from under the chair to end up by trying to leap onto April's lap. All in all, Thornton gave a very impressive display for such a young dog.

Clay appeared to be embarrassed by what was going on, and April looked as if she was about to start crying.

"Clay please, have a seat. April, please sit all the way back on your chair and keep your hands off Thornton. Here, read these directions, and Clay if you would fill out this form for me." After handing out the necessary paperwork, I sat back to watch.

Thornton was really quite amazing in the number of different behaviors he had available to him that all showed just how displeased he happened to be at the moment. He would run through the entire repertoire, stop, look at Clay, try to get on April's lap, and then glare at me. Next would follow a five-minute period of silence before the entire act would start up once more. Truly amazing. There were just no other words for his abilities other than amazing.

Once we were pretty much settled, I was able to both ask questions of them and answer their questions. Preliminary questions out of the way, I picked up one of my ecollars, explained how it worked and gave them both of them a chance to test it on themselves. While we were busy Thornton was lunging, screaming, trying to eat the chair leg, trying to climb on April and barking. After about 20 minutes of this behavior he settled into what I think of as cadence barking. You know what I mean. Even if you have never owned a dog, I'm willing to bet you have heard cadence barking. It is possibly the most annoying type of barking of all. Bark, bark, bark, pause for a beat of 3 and then bark, bark, bark, pause for a beat of 3, well you get my meaning.

Once a dog starts cadence barking, you know you are in for a long haul because this is a bark that can and will go on for hours if something doesn't step in and stop it. I had just the tool; and since I had already put an ecollar on Thornton, all I had to do was pick up the correct remote and start looking for the right level.

The first time I pushed the button, nothing happened. I clicked to a higher level and pushed again. Again our only reward was bark, bark, bark, pause, bark. I clicked up another level and then another. Finally Thornton went bark, bark, pause. He looked around, cocked his head and gave a bark. I pushed the button. He scratched his neck and looked puzzled. Another single bark, but I swear this one had a question mark after it. I pushed the button again. Silence.

April and Clay both looked at me, then back at Thornton, and then back at me. I just smiled and didn't say a word. The silence started to stretch and so did Thornton. Stretch, I mean. He stretched, yawned, sniffed the floor, found a spot to suit him, and lay down. End of cadence barking, end of lunging, end of biting the chair leg, end of screaming, screeching and hurling himself around. Slowly the tension in the air slid out through the crack under the closed door. Now we would be able to talk in quiet, relaxed tones. This new silence was so much better, and all thanks to my favorite training tool.

"Okay, guys, you have now seen just what sort of magic an ecollar is able to produce. What is more, Thornton is now showing you he can be relaxed and maintain self-control. Shall we take a stroll outside and see just what else Thornton is able to do?"

"How did you…" April started to say.

"…Do that?" Clay finished for her.

"You saw it. All I did was find Thornton's response level. Then I pushed the button on the remote each time he barked. Everything else was up to him. You saw just how fast he figured out how to control the ecollar. Do you realize he has been doing the very same thing to the both of you? The control part, I mean."

"We do now." Said in unison.

"Good. Now the next thing Thornton is going to learn is how to walk through a doorway in a polite manner." And so the lesson went. Thornton was a quick study and figured things out probably faster than either April or Clay (which was more than likely why they were in trouble to begin with).

After the lesson was over, the Stadd's left without making another appointment. I wasn't really surprised, since I had been sensing April's reluctance to be serious with Thornton's training. Ah well, even the single lesson would have some positive effect on Thorn's behavior.

Three days later I heard from Clay. His voice was so distraught when I first answered the phone I wasn't sure it was the Clay Stadd that had been here just a few days earlier.

Seems dear Thornton had gone and done it again. Out the front door and on a merry chase through the neighborhood leaving a trail of screams, angry yells and another broken lamp in his wake. They were ready to schedule a full set of lessons and of course they wanted to start at once.

As a sort of postscript, yes, they did learn to use an electronic collar. Yes, Thorn did learn to come when called. He learned to stay in one spot when told. He learned to walk on a leash without pulling. He learned to go to a designated place and stay there until released. Then at my insistence, they taught him a trick. That one trick earned him a special place in everyone's hearts and earned the Stadds a welcome at the neighborhood summer block parties.

About the Author

Margot Woods has been training dogs professionally for more than 30 years. She is a member of the International Association of Canine Professionals, the Metropolitan Baltimore Doberman Pinscher Club, the founder of a local assistance dog training organization, and serves on the Citizen's Advisory Committee for Persons with Disabilities for the city of Laurel, Maryland. She is the owner of an active email list known as Balanced Trainers that can be found on Yahoo.com.

She presently lives in Laurel with her son, Jesse and a Doberman known far and wide as Wrap The Alien. Her web page may be viewed by going to www.applewoodsdogtraining.com. Mud Heaven is her first full-length book.